Alphas Undone Book 1

KENDALL RYAN

About the Book

Love is a trap, a trick only other people fall for. Former Navy SEAL Nolan Maxwell has no such illusions. The only things real in his life are his beloved bulldog and the two women who regularly share his bed. One is light—soft, innocent, and tender touches. The other is dark—and gives him all the wicked things he craves behind closed doors. It's not cheating when each is aware of the other. But when he begins to feel much more than he ever bargained for, the order of his carefully crafted world is shaken, and he stands to lose everything.

Nolan thinks we met by chance. We didn't. I sought him out, seduced him, and in return got the sanctuary I needed to survive. But now, impossibly, I've fallen in love with him. I don't care that he has another lover, because when he finds out who I am, it's going to ruin any chance I ever had with him anyway. She's the least of my worries.

Bait & Switch is Book 1 in a new contemporary romance series by Kendall Ryan.

Prologue

Knowing how much her curves affected him, she used them to her full advantage. Standing before the floor-length mirror in her bedroom, she lifted her breasts so the cups of her bra cradled them nice and high. *There.*

She gave a little wiggle in the mirror. Black leggings and a low-cut red tunic hugged the curves of her hips while still emphasizing her trim waist. She smiled at her own reflection, something dark and possessive flashing in her eyes, her mouth curling into a bloodthirsty grin.

She wanted him to pant like a dog when he saw her. No more of this sharing bullshit. She might have said she was okay with it in the beginning, but that had been a lie. One meant to soothe and calm his worries, win him over. And she had.

Tonight she would show him, despite her many faults, that all he needed was right in front of him. Two damaged souls with murky pasts who were perfect for each other.

Nearly overcome with anticipation, she scurried around her bedroom, tossing stray clothes into the closet and fluffing her pillows for the third time. He would be here any minute, and she'd been looking forward to this moment all day.

Glancing at her dresser, she wondered if the red pillar candles she'd lit were too much. He wasn't much for romance, but she didn't care. Tonight she was going to make him hers. It had been too long, and her body was almost humming with need for him. She wanted him to fill her and mark her skin, just as he'd marked her heart.

Her bare feet paused at the wool throw rug beside her bed as something shifted inside her. *Should I feel guilty?*

She was escaping a dark past . . . but it was light that cast the greatest shadow.

Swallowing the bitter taste of acid in her mouth, she shook her head. There was no way she was backing down now. Everything about him made her feel alive, raw, and visceral. She wanted him. All of him.

Hearts would be broken. Secrets would be revealed. And nothing would ever be the same.

Chapter One

Nolan

The black leather ball gag went on first. I brushed aside Daniella's wavy auburn hair to fasten its buckle, snapping my fingers for her to open her mouth and accept it. I stepped forward to tighten the straps, my body lingering against hers for longer than necessary. Her stiffened nipples brushed my bare chest and my cock answered, already half-hard, nudging at her through my jeans.

I'd ordered her to stand motionless unless I said otherwise. But I made the task as difficult for her as possible. Every time she fidgeted, even slightly, I spanked her naked ass hard with my open palm. She shuddered and earned another slap. Her creamy skin had started to redden, her breath coming faster.

She didn't really need the gag. If I told her to be quiet, she would have done her best. This little ritual was all about heightening her anticipation.

"On the bed," I finally commanded, my voice low and gruff. "All fours, hands and feet. Show me your pretty cunt." I might have sounded cool and in control, but my own heart was pounding just as hard and fast as hers.

Her breathing hitched, and I fought down a smile.

After leaving the Navy SEALs two years ago, an unfamiliar feeling of powerlessness had swirled inside me. The realization that no one needed me, no one was waiting on my command, had been a tough pill to swallow. And even though I'd been more than ready to leave it all behind, I found I hated my new life on the outside.

But then Daniella needed me, needed me to be the man to save her. So I made that my mission.

I didn't remember my military years fondly, but for the sake of satisfying Daniella's hunger, I recaptured that military air of authority. Power, punishment, strict control ... I needed this almost as badly as she did. The high that came from playing this role was like nothing else. And judging by the way she hustled onto the bed, eager to please, my performance was a good one.

Daniella grabbed her ankles and prostrated herself with her head down and ass raised high.

Jesus Christ. My cock immediately sprang to full attention. Since a delay would just make her squirm with more anticipation, I let myself pause to stare. Tight ass with a slick, flushed pussy pouting below. Mile-long legs, shapely from all the hours she spent on her feet as a nurse. Ripe, firm tits with pale, pierced nipples. Hair spread dark over the white pillow, gleaming copper where it caught the light. Pale, freckle-dusted skin, decorated with a few swirling tribal tattoos.

Well, it was about to be decorated with a hell of a lot more.

I rolled on the condom she'd set out on her nightstand and pulled out a coil of silk rope. I climbed onto the bed behind her to tie her wrists to her ankles; she liked to be bound as tight as possible. Then I got on my knees, letting my steel-hard cock rub her wet pussy, teasing her mercilessly. She whimpered and tried to rock back into me.

I'd been waiting for her to do something like that. "Bad girl," I barked. "I decide when you get fucked." I spanked her firmly, open-palmed.

She yelped, only to choke when I spanked her again, again, and again, raising fiery streaks of crimson across her ass. I stopped when she sobbed for breath, knowing she was overwhelmed with that mysterious feeling she craved, neither pain nor pleasure but something more. Something she couldn't get anywhere else. Something I alone gave her.

I grabbed her hips, digging my fingers in, and thrust forward, filling her inch by glorious inch. A moan of animal greed clawed up from deep in Daniella's chest. I pulled back all the way and pounded in again, setting a punishing pace.

My hips smacked audibly against her flaming ass. She cried out again when I bent forward over her arched back and sank my teeth into her nape, marking her every way I could.

She thrashed to ride me, pushing back on my cock with what little leverage she had. Soon her guttural cries took on a familiar note of desperation. Panting with effort and pleasure, still biting the back of her neck, I let go of one hip to rub her clit. She almost screamed, and her pussy gripped hard, milking me. I groaned at the sensation; she must have been teetering on the edge since we started.

I fucked Daniella through her orgasm until she trembled with overstimulation. But I didn't stop there. I couldn't—my own release was coming hard and fast.

I kept moving my fingers as she squirmed, torn between jerking away from my touch and pressing closer. The heat in my belly built higher with every thrust. Just as it broke, her toes curled and she cried out weakly, coming again.

Fuck. My cock throbbed hard, and I growled out a curse. *Damn, that was good.*

Still buried deep inside her, I unbuckled the wet ball gag and let it drop from Daniella's mouth. She gave a breathy, satisfied noise, working her tired jaw as I pulled out and sat back on my heels to untie her slim ankles.

She rolled over onto her side, hugging her knees to her chest, her eyes still closed and expression relaxed. Once I'd pulled off the condom and threw it away, I grabbed the cashmere throw from the back of her desk chair and covered her with it. She lay there quietly, her breathing evening out while I sat beside her.

Lifting one side of the blanket, I inspected my work. Her right ass cheek was red and warm to the touch. That would fade in a few hours, but damn, sitting wouldn't be comfortable tonight. This was the part I didn't care for. Guilt mixed with bitter uncertainty over what I'd done, making me wonder if I'd taken it too far.

"Roll over. Onto your stomach," I told her. *Too stern.* I swallowed and worked on letting go of the dominance still coursing through my veins.

"I'm fine, Nolan. I promise." Even as she protested, Daniella obeyed.

I took a bottle of soothing oatmeal lotion from her nightstand. "I know." Pushing aside my own guilt, I uncovered her and rubbed the lotion over the welts, taking my time to cover every inch of her bright pink ass, touching her gently so as not to cause her more discomfort.

She let out a contented sigh. "That was . . ."

"You have a good time?" I asked, only a trace of a smirk

on my lips.

She turned her head on the pillow, one hazel eye crinkled in amusement. "Are you fishing for compliments?" Once our scene was over, it was crazy how quickly we fell back into casual friend territory.

"Hey, a man wants to know he's done his job."

Although I already knew damn well I had. She still hadn't budged from her spot, which meant I must have worn her out. Or she was savoring her journey out of subspace. I capped the lotion and pulled the blanket back over her, my work done.

"So you *were* fishing for compliments," she teased. But there was no real venom in her low voice. She still sounded hazy, her high not yet faded. Soon she would be just plain old relaxed. "Of course you're the best fuck I've ever had."

I chuckled as I freed her from the last knots. "Now that's what I want to hear."

Daniella scooted back to sit up against the headboard, tugging the blanket with her. I handed her the granola bar and thermos of black coffee I'd prepared earlier. She tore into her snack while I rubbed her shoulders.

We fucked like this at least once or twice a week, which was fine by me. Her shifts were always changing, but I knew her general workday pattern by now. Slave away at the hospital for twelve hours, come home, drop dead, wake up hungry and horny. One kink session would soothe and refresh her nerves; two would knock her out again.

Once Daniella seemed okay, I kissed the back of her hand and left to take a boiling-hot, soapy shower. I was meeting Lacey soon, and she probably wouldn't appreciate me reeking of sweat and sex. Some women were into that, but I wasn't going to bet on it.

Especially not with this one.

I thought back to last Saturday night as I scrubbed myself. When I first saw Lacey at the dive bar, she had seemed so innocent and out of place. But despite her modest casual clothes and scant makeup, she didn't quite fit the girl-next-door type. She was too striking—her features too fine, her eyes too big and crystalline blue, her dark hair the color of chocolate too long and sleek.

And even as she'd flirted, smiling shyly, enticingly, there had been something solemn about her. Something she held back. It only made me want to dig in and find out. Maybe it was my line of work, but a question deserved an answer.

When Lacey told me she was new in town, I'd offered up my number in case she ever needed anything. Plus, I just wanted to fend off the horny, opportunistic vultures circling her. Moving from one city to another was always hard, especially for a woman alone. But I didn't imagine I was fooling anyone with any ideas about my chivalry. She was a hot piece of ass and I wanted to fuck her, simple as that.

And even though Lacey looked like a goody-two-shoes, she'd made it clear that she was interested. A few days ago, she'd texted to ask if I wanted to grab a drink.

I'd said sure, knowing Daniella wouldn't mind. We had talked a long time ago about what we wanted out of our relationship. We were there for each other in a unique way. It worked. Perfectly, in fact.

After what Daniella had been through, her first priority was stability, and once she was safe, having her sexual needs met was a close second. Romance—let alone monogamy—didn't even make the list. Two years ago, Daniella's last Dom had ended their five-year relationship by kicking her out and replacing her with a younger sub.

I'd been at the right place at the right time and invited her to crash at my place. This house was too big for just me, anyway, and my job paid plenty, so I was able to take care of her every need. Physically and emotionally. She took on more than her fair share of cooking and cleaning—I'd never asked her to, but she didn't want to feel like a charity case, so in a sense she took care of me too, I supposed.

And since I definitely wasn't looking for love either, we were a good match. With no interest in messy entanglements that could lead to commitment, I ensured my world didn't involve heartache. Two distinct events had led me here, and the six years I spent on the world's deadliest battlegrounds sealed the deal. I only wanted easy, good times from here on out.

I lived in the moment, and right now, my mission was to enjoy life without getting tied down. Take advantage of my newfound freedom away from the military. Screw whatever women caught my eye. I gave Daniella what she needed to feel safe and satisfied, and in return, I had a live-in fuck buddy to take the edge off whenever I needed it. Daniella was a broken woman who was learning to be herself again, and knew how to have fun ... in more ways than the usual roommate. We had worked hard to get our relationship to where we were today.

I left the bathroom, not bothering to wrap a towel around me. Daniella had finished resting and was getting dressed. She glanced at me as I passed her bedroom, idly curious, now in her black satin bra and panties.

"You on your way somewhere?"

"I'm going to meet Lacey in half an hour," I replied,

pausing at the door to watch two sets of Daniella's curves—one in the flesh, the other in the closet door's mirror.

She ogled my muscular, naked body, her eyes drawn down to my generous cock, and I couldn't help but smirk. I knew she liked what she saw, along with nearly every woman in our small Texas town. But a little female appreciation never got old.

Finally, she laughed and broke our staring match to put on her tank top. "You're helping her unpack right now? It's kind of late."

"Not right now. We're having a drink."

Daniella hummed, giving me knowing smile. "Oh, I see. Pussy patrol."

I grunted in acknowledgment. With Lacey, I doubted it was going to be so easy, but that was the general idea.

"Is she a frog hog?" Daniella shimmied into her baby-blue scrubs.

I didn't much care for that term, but it was commonly used to describe women who chased after Navy SEALs strictly for the bragging rights.

"I don't think so. Even if she is, I'm a few years past the expiration date." And thank fucking God for that. Six years of ground-pounding in the world's hottest crisis zones had been more than enough misery. I did my time, and had the battle scars to prove it.

Daniella shrugged. "Those girls don't give a shit. All they hear is *Navy SEAL* and their panties drop to their ankles."

"Not that there's anything wrong with that," I said, lips twitching upward. After all, I'd had my share of fun with tag chasers before I quit the service. *Why the fuck not?*

"Nah, of course not. Just seems like a lot of competition for . . . what, two thousand guys in the whole world?" She brushed her hair in quick, hard strokes and tied it up in a high ponytail. "Anyway, if you're going on the prowl tonight, I think I'll grab a quick bite with the girls before we carpool to the hospital."

I chuckled at the mental image—a gaggle of pastel-clad nurses invading the greasy spoon around the corner. "You want me to drive you?"

"On your way to the bar? Where you'll be drinking? With another woman? Hell no. Wouldn't want to impose on your *date*." She waved me away. "Now, stop staring at my ass and go have fun. You're going to be late unless you get going soon."

"Christ, woman, sometimes I wonder if you're really submissive."

With a wicked grin, she turned toward me and held up

her arms, showing the not-quite-faded marks on her wrists. "*This* is all the proof I need."

I couldn't argue with that. Daniella had an insatiable appetite for rough sex—biting and clawing, spanking and paddling, nipple clamps, hot wax, butt plugs, and especially bondage. Everything I knew about BDSM, I had learned from her.

Knowing that she was right and I needed to get moving, I headed down the hall to my own bedroom. When I opened the door, the fat English bulldog on my bed woke up with a wheezy snort. One look at me and he started grumbling for attention.

"Hey there, buddy," I said, rubbing his wrinkled back. "Have a nice nap?"

Sutton stared up at me dolefully. He was lying so flat that his face was sunken almost entirely into his jowls.

"Sorry, man. It's gotta be this way."

I'd learned to shut Sutton in his bedroom while Daniella and I were playing. She wasn't fond of the drooling, farting beast, and a cold wet nose on the ass would kill anyone's mood. So I always coddled and reassured Sutton afterward to make up for the missed attention.

After a few minutes of my petting and praising him with

a steady stream of nonsense talk, the old dog was grinning and wiggling like a puppy. I finished with a couple of hard pats on the flank, and then swept my hand in a *shoo* gesture.

"Okay, now go. I need to get the hell out of here."

Sutton jumped off the bed with a heavy thud. He lumbered into the living room, favoring his bad hip, puffing and blowing as he tottered along unevenly.

As I got dressed for a night out, my thoughts drifted back to Lacey.

• • •

West's Watering Hole wasn't a swanky joint. It was the kind of casual place you came when you wanted a stiff drink and to relax among the local twenty-somethings. No frills. No fuss. Metal bar stools and wood floors, and low lighting to keep the mood relaxed.

I nodded at my friend and former teammate, West, who was playing barback tonight. He blended in so seamlessly with the bar staff, you'd never guess he owned the place.

West tipped his head, acknowledging me with a grunt. He was a grumpy ass, but I was guessing that a woman—or two—could help take that scowl off his face. That was something West would have to figure out on his own, though. No sense getting my boxers in a twist over another man's problems.

From the quiet corner where I'd grabbed a table for two, I ventured a glance to the door. Lacey was standing there, her eyes wide as her gaze wandered the room. When I rose to my feet, she spotted me and darted over. I took a moment to appreciate the view as she approached. Soft porcelain skin, shiny dark hair, a tight little body I wanted to hold down and fuck.

She looked up at that moment, and I was thankful the pornographic images playing through my brain weren't being broadcast through the bar. Every guy in here had noticed her, which was evidenced by the sudden hush when she passed the pool tables, and the heads turning as she walked by. Lacey was a bombshell, but in a quiet, girl-next-door sort of way.

Grinning stupidly, I accepted her hand when she neared and pulled her in for a hug. She smelled incredible.

"Thanks for meeting me tonight," she murmured, her voice soft, her gaze resting at my feet.

Damn, she was gorgeous. "'Course, sweetheart."

Her eyes found mine as she slid into her seat. It was a good thing I'd already ordered us drinks, remembering her preferences from the first time we'd met, because her smile left me speechless.

There was something captivating about the woman.

It wasn't just her petite hourglass build, or the way her gaze drifted away from mine when she spoke of her past, or the curious way she watched me over the rim of her margarita glass. No, it wasn't something I could put my finger on, which made me all the more interested. She was a walking contradiction. A bright smile and sweet personality, but with a secret darkness lingering in her eyes. Sharp and inquisitive, yet naive. Kind, yet guarded.

Even her name suited her in a weird way. *Lacey.* Something delicate and intricate, pure white, beautiful because of the skill and patience it demanded. Something that could be damaged or destroyed if you weren't careful.

We'd covered all the basics the first time we met. She was twenty-three, originally from Oklahoma. I was twenty-seven, a Texas boy born and bred. She had one younger sister, while I was an only child. My SEAL teammates were the only brothers I needed.

"What did you do today?" she asked.

I filled her in on my volunteer work with the troubled-teen camp about an hour and a half outside of Dallas.

"This kid Martinez is so close, you know? If he pushed himself, if he really *believed*, he'd have the chance at an athletic scholarship. He'd do damn fine in the military too. And he doesn't see it."

"Your work there sounds very gratifying."

I smirked at her. "It is. When I can get the little pencil-dicks to listen."

She laughed and took another sip of her icy drink, her eyes lingering on mine over the rim of the glass. It seemed she liked what she saw—and not just the outside package, like most women. She admired *me*, my work. It felt . . . *nice*.

If I were smarter, I might have been on high alert about why she was suddenly here in this small town, batting those fuck-me eyes at me. My cock, however, didn't give a flying fuck about such things. I wanted to be buried six ways from Sunday inside this gorgeous new woman. And with any luck, I would be.

But my situation required a little more finesse than most men's. I had absolutely no plans to change my arrangement with Daniella, and Lacey didn't seem like the type for one-night stands or booty calls.

The contrast between them made my cock ache. Daniella was tall and elegant and tranquil—at least, until bondage unleashed her wild side. Lacey was little and restless and curvy under her unassuming clothes. I imagined picking her up like a toy and fucking her against a wall. I'd traded grueling SEAL workouts for a more reasonable routine, but my body was still cut to rival any gym rat's, and I would be able to hold up Lacey through orgasm after orgasm. Until she sagged in my arms, finally calm.

The two women couldn't have been more different. Where one was dark, with her ravenous sexual cravings and wicked pleasures, the other was light with her innocent smile and guarded reactions. But she still had that gleam in her eye like she was interested in a little fun.

What would she feel like, her small, voluptuous body moving over mine as she rode my thick length? Would she rock slowly back and forth, or bounce on me hard and fast? Would she make soft mewling whimpers or scream out her pleasure?

"What about you? Do you live alone?" Lacey was asking.

I hadn't been paying attention. Was she implying that she wanted to go back to my place?

I shook my head, more at myself than her. *Fuck, man, slow down.* I needed to rein in my libido. If I didn't concentrate on the conversation here, the real Lacey would never turn into my naked, writhing fantasy.

"No, I've got one roommate," I replied. "But she works weird hours, so I have the place to myself a lot."

"Did you say *she*?" After a moment's pause, Lacey asked, "Is she your . . . friend?"

I knew what she really wanted to ask, and I wasn't ashamed of the answer. So it was high time to cut to the chase and give her full disclosure.

"Sort of. Our situation is unconventional," I said. "We *are* friends . . . who also sleep together sometimes. But we're not exclusive."

Lacey blinked, her expression unreadable. Was she offended? Disgusted? Or was she just startled and taking a minute to process everything?

"I'm telling you this so there's no confusion or hurt feelings down the road. If you're not interested in me anymore, I understand completely. But Daniella's an important part of my life."

Another slow, big-eyed blink. Just as I started preparing for her to freak out, she replied, "So long as you don't expect me to have a threesome, we're cool." And then she sipped at her margarita, as casual as could be.

My eyebrows raised slightly. *Well, hell.* That had gone better than expected. The good girl just kept on surprising me. But despite her airy tone, I could tell she had opinions that she was keeping to herself.

"Tell me what you're thinking, Lacey," I said, my tone leaving no room for negotiation.

The last thing I wanted was a lover who acted chill, trying to be someone she wasn't, until she couldn't keep a lid on her resentment anymore.

Chapter Two

Lacey

Taking a sip of my margarita, I fought to maintain a neutral expression, even while my stomach had jumped into my throat and the lime from my drink burned like acid on my tongue.

When the dangerously sexy man seated before me admitted that he had another lover, my first instinct was to abort. *Run*, common sense demanded. The restless side of me, however, was willing to hear him out.

An open relationship was not conventional in my world. Things like this didn't happen where I was from. At least, not that I was aware of. But I wasn't looking for a boyfriend, or even monogamy. So I put on my best *open-minded* expression and listened to what he had to say.

Hearing him talk about her, though, it was clear that she had a special place in his life. I didn't understand it yet, but the woman obviously filled a unique role.

"Tell me what you're thinking, Lacey," Nolan said.

My name on his lips was like a soft plea. There was no way I could lie to him—at least, not about this—even if I'd wanted to. He was every bit the firm-tempered alpha male I dreamed he might be. Former military special forces, decorated in combat, and now a civilian, but certainly not soft.

"It's an unusual arrangement, but as long as you're up front with everything, I don't see any harm." I didn't know if my words were the complete truth, but who was I to judge his situation? I had plenty of baggage of my own.

I supposed it was no different from most casual dating situations these days. Men and woman often explored various relationships, multiple partners before settling down, and at least Nolan wasn't doing it behind anyone's back.

As I watched him take another sip of his drink, I couldn't stop my mind from wandering to illicit things. Like the way his strong arms might feel around me, the way his lips might feel on mine. The intensity rolling off him in waves, even his scent—the perfect combination of cologne and mild soap—made my heart beat like a drum.

"And all of this, it's . . . cool with her? Your friend, I mean." I stumbled over my words, my lack of experience with the situation shining through.

"Daniella is definitely *cool* with me having other fucks, yes." He chuckled softly, as if I'd missed some inside joke or dark reference. "But something tells me you're not a one-night, fuck-hard-and-leave type of girl."

I swallowed, my throat tightening as his words washed over me. The *leave* part, not so much, but the *fuck hard* part . . . that sounded pretty good right now.

"No, I guess I'm not. If there's enough passion and connection between two people, why should it end at one night?"

Setting down his now-empty glass of whiskey, Nolan leaned closer. His expression was amused. "Looking at you, I couldn't agree more. I haven't properly dated in a long damn time, but you have me . . . intrigued."

"So we'll take it slow. Friends," I added. There was no sense rushing into this. I needed time to feel him out. Make sure I had done the right thing by coming here.

"Might be hard to be friends with someone I want under me."

I blinked at him.

"I want you in my bed, Lacey. No use denying it." His thumb slid across the rim of his glass, the movement innocent, yet suggestive at the same time.

After I got over the initial shock of his blunt words, I appreciated his straightforward attitude. The man certainly didn't try to hide things.

"What makes you think I'm ever going to be in your

bed?" I asked, my gaze steady and holding his.

"I know what you're doing," he murmured.

"What's that?"

He leaned closer, placing his elbows on the table, invading more of my space. "Playing hard to get. You know as well as I do that men like the chase."

"So you're really just a predator. No better than a caveman."

His gaze cut through me like a knife. "Instinct tells us to seek, hunt, and—"

"Fuck," I interrupted, knowing full well what was on his mind. The bar's warm atmosphere and the tequila coursing through my veins had apparently loosened my tongue.

"Exactly, Lacey. It's nature. Not a thing I can do about it." The hint of humor in his voice kept me from arguing my point further.

"Uh-huh," I simply supplied.

It seemed that the man who volunteered his weekends to help troubled teens had quite the dirty mouth. I was starting to glimpse his many sides, and I wanted to uncover more of those contrasts and angles. I could honestly say I'd never met a man like him.

He smiled at me and signaled to our waitress for another

round. "So, what is it that you do?"

It was strange how we knew so little about each other, yet our connection already felt as deep and wide as the Mississippi. Tension and interest crackled between us, just out of reach.

"I'm the new part-time assistant at the animal shelter across town. The pay isn't great and the hours kind of suck, but I enjoy it."

The cheery tone in my voice disguised my disenchantment. I loved animals, and I was happy to have a job there, but the ten dollars an hour and facility that constantly smelled of poop was a far cry from my previous life.

I'd graduated with a degree in finance last year and landed at a great firm straight out of school, making good money. I'd worn designer suits, treated myself to pedicures and silky lingerie, escaped winter's doldrums with extravagant beach vacations. I'd dreamed of working my way up to finance manager. But all that was on hold for the time being.

It was just money, I reminded myself. I had everything I needed to live, and no more.

"An animal lover?" he asked.

"Guilty," I said, smiling.

Nolan shook his head, chuckling. "I'm not allowed back in that place." At my confused expression, he continued. "It's more of a self-imposed ban. I adopted Sutton two years ago, but could have easily left with as many dogs and cats as would have fit into my truck."

I knew just what he meant. All the animals there deserved a good home. "And what's Sutton like?" I asked, my curiosity piqued.

"He's an English bulldog. Ornery as shit, missing a few teeth, and he has a bad hip, but he's mine."

I warmed at the image. So far, Nolan had been anything but what I was expecting. A bit presumptuous and rough around the edges, lacking the discipline I might have expected from an ex-SEAL. By his own account, he was living life according to his brain's pleasure center. Women. Whiskey. And apparently a penchant for bulldogs. That last thought made me smile.

"What do you like to do in your free time?" he asked, drawing me back to the moment.

I shrugged. "Nothing too crazy. Decorating my place with unique flea-market finds . . . silk throw pillows, pretty black and white prints. I enjoy hunting out forgotten treasures like that. Oh, and I love college football. I went to Oklahoma, so . . ." I hid a smirk, knowing their huge rivalry with Texas.

He scrubbed a hand across his face. "Don't tell me you're a Sooners fan?"

I grinned back at him. It was too easy. "You think I'm going to automatically root for the Longhorns just because I moved to Texas?"

"No, I'd expect you to root for them because they're the best damn team in the country."

That made me chuckle. I knew what people saw when they looked at me. A fresh face with only minimal makeup, a long chocolate-colored braid hanging over one shoulder, a pair of faded jeans, a conservative cotton top that didn't show even a hint of cleavage. He probably had me pegged as a stereotypical good girl.

Something inside me wanted to prove him wrong, to show him I was not only okay with his situation, but open and curious. Prove to him that whatever he could dish out, I could take it.

Still, I couldn't blame him for how I must have seemed. My entire appearance screamed innocence and propriety. It was the way I'd been raised. As the only child of a single, very old-fashioned father, modesty had been drilled into me from a young age, and there was nothing I could do to change it now. Which was fine.

This was the way I was most comfortable anyhow, and it had never stopped me from attracting male attention before. But as I glanced around at the women in the bar, with their low-cut sequined tops and sling-back heels, I realized Nolan could have his pick of the litter. And there were clearly more enticing choices than me, yet his eyes didn't wander, his gaze didn't stray from mine even once. It sent a warm ripple of pleasure down my spine.

"Maybe we'll catch a game sometime," he offered. His voice was low and laced with suggestion.

"Maybe we will." I lowered my gaze to my salt-rimmed glass on the table, wondering exactly what might unfold with this mystery man in the coming weeks.

From his broad shoulders to his *don't fuck with me or mine* attitude, everything about him screamed protector. I had grown up idolizing my father, thinking that his defining traits—stoic, dutiful, protective, dominant—were what made the perfect man.

Seeing those same qualities in Nolan lit something inside me. It was more than admiration, if the sudden pounding of my heart was any indication. Raw heat radiated between us. His conversation might have been casual, but the amusement in his eyes as he watched me was provocative and sexual. My body answered with a hearty *hell yeah*, my panties dampening as I shifted in my seat.

"Come on, let's get out of here." Nolan reached for my hand, and I placed my palm against his in silent agreement.

Common sense flying out the window, I was going to ride this wave and see where it took me.

Chapter Three

Nolan

I hadn't been here in years, and I was pretty sure I hadn't brought a woman up here since my senior year of high school. Even though it was the type of place that would be sure to get a woman in the mood. I told myself I just didn't want to wake Daniella, but part of me wondered if maybe I wanted Lacey all to myself. That, and I knew she'd be the type of woman to want to take things slow. This was my attempt at making tonight count as two dates.

Back then, if my parents had caught me sneaking a girl into my bedroom, it would have meant I was benched from football and given enough extra chores on the ranch to occupy all my free time. Which was why I'd lost my virginity here when I was seventeen. The place held some sentimental value. I was an only child, and my parent's expectations were sky high. Probably how I ended up in the military. Discipline and hard work were bred into me from a young age.

"Where are we going?" Lacey's small hand tightened around mine as she trotted along behind me in the moonlight.

"Not much further."

I remembered each step like it was yesterday. The huge boulders resting against the side of the hill created a rocky cliff, the valley down below quiet and still. Far in the distance, lights twinkled in the darkness.

"Oh wow." Lacey stopped behind me. "Is that downtown?"

I nodded. It was a pretty view. The peaceful stillness of the country contrasted sharply with the city lights, many miles away.

"After I retired from the military, this is where I came some sleepless nights. Just to think. And sit in the quiet," I told her. It was also where I came when I was feeling sorry for myself, and to mourn everything I'd lost. But most of that was behind me now.

"Would you like to sit?" I motioned to the large outcrop that hung over the valley below.

"Sure."

She took my hand again and I led her to the spot where the rock dipped down, creating the perfect ledge. The evening air was cool, as was the stone through our jeans, and Lacey nestled herself against my side. When I placed my arm around her small frame, she settled in beside me.

We talked about bands we liked, concerts we'd seen, and

favorite movies without any awkward silences. It was fucking weird, actually. I hadn't taken the time to just get to know a woman like this in a long time. Typically, if I left West's with a woman, we were fucking within minutes. And within an hour, I was back home and in the shower. Alone.

I liked listening to Lacey talk. Her voice held no twang, despite her upbringing. It was sweet and soft and smoky. *Intoxicating.* I'd lost my accent in the military. Figured I couldn't sound like the tough negotiator I wanted to be with a good-ole-boy accent.

"Do you travel much for work?" she asked, drawing me out of my thoughts.

"Not too much. A night or two occasionally is about the extent of it."

She nodded as if that pleased her somehow. "So you haven't dated anyone seriously ... I mean, been monogamous in a long time?"

"Nope."

"I see."

She knew damn well there was a story there, but wasn't going to press me for it right now. *Good girl.*

I knew I was emotionally crippled. I knew my limits, knew that all I could offer was physical exploration. Maybe friendship. Certainly nothing more. But with this woman, something felt different. She was warm and soft beside me, and she wanted to hear me talk about my background, my family. She was even curious about Daniella, but kept her questions fairly neutral.

"Thanks for bringing me out here. It's beautiful, and it's nice to get some fresh air." She drew a big inhale. "Things were kind of rushed when I moved, and the only places I've seen have been the inside of my apartment and where I work." She shifted beside me. "Haven't even had a normal conversation in weeks."

"Not running from the law, are you?" I asked, looking over at her in the moonlight.

Her gaze swung out toward the valley, and I took a moment to just watch her. The slope of her cheek. Her full, lush mouth. The slender column of her throat. She was stunning.

"Why, would that be a deal breaker for you?" She turned, smiling at me, but there was something sad in her eyes.

"We've all done some shit we're not proud of."

I looked out into the distance below. Her battle wounds might not be visible, but I sensed they were there, lurking under the surface just like mine.

I still didn't have a handle on what was going on here, but temptation whispered to me over the rush of her heartbeat. It was crazy that even knowing it might not end well, I wanted her.

I left nothing to chance in my professional life; every possible scenario was accounted for. So why did I have the feeling my personal life was about to go sideways?

For now, I let myself soak in the silence. Her head rested on my shoulder, and we listened to the wind rustle the tall grasses below.

Chapter Four

Nolan

I set up the conference room's projector as the rest of Redstone's employees filed in. All fourteen of them were veterans, about half former Special Operations. I felt at home in the testosterone-packed atmosphere, but sometimes I wished my job featured a little more eye candy and a little less machismo.

Not everyone had left their military rivalries behind. Cocky taunts and trash-talking were the norm. Mixing a roomful of former SEALs, retired police officers, and ex-Delta Force was delicate enough, but when you added in the guys who bled the mantra *once a Marine, always a Marine*, forget about it.

I didn't understand why people hung on to their old identities, anyway. As far as I was concerned, I'd be happy if I never heard another *hooyah!* ever again. And Jerry Barton, my current boss and former SEAL team leader, had evidently felt the same way. Commander Barton had walked away from a promising officer career to start his own private security firm as a civilian.

I might have been sitting in a conference room, but as I

waited for the meeting to begin, my mind wandered right back to that evening with Lacey. The curious way she watched me, her eyes wide with wonder and attraction. The luscious curves hidden under her modest clothing that I couldn't wait to rip away. The sadness hidden in her eyes when she spoke of her background. It made me want to gather her up and fix whatever had put that frown on her face.

Deep down, I knew I should leave her alone. She was a nice girl. Sweet. Unspoiled. But I had no intention of walking away. Not because I lacked discipline, but because it would be way too much fun to have her. Under me. On top of me. And these days, my life was all about taking what I wanted, when I wanted it. I'd learned the hard way that you never knew when you might draw your last breath.

The screen flickered on and filled with Barton's stern, weathered face, snapping me out of my erotic daydream. He'd been leading the weekly company meetings by video chat, since he was busy in DC for the rest of the quarter. All chatter in the room died instantly. Their founder was roughly fifty-five years old, but the only thing that gave it away was his salt-and-pepper hair; he was fitter and trimmer than most men half his age, the picture of discipline.

"Good morning, gentlemen," Barton announced. "I trust

you've all reviewed my e-mail about this week's available contracts."

Everyone nodded. Nobody on earth had balls big enough to ignore one of Barton's dictates.

"I'll be happy to coordinate the team's preferences and e-mail them back to you later this morning," Greyson offered.

Many of the jobs listed had been on the table before. Guarding the same corporate bigwigs, helping law enforcement conduct advanced intelligence training, consulting with state agencies on counter-terrorism techniques. Repeat business from faithful customers.

Barton lifted his chin to the side. "I'll review and approve it later today. I have intel on something new that I'm not quite ready to share with the team." His eyes cut over to mine and lingered there.

Interesting.

Barton had an expert sense of which jobs matched best with which team members. But to keep everyone happy with their schedules, he always presented his opinions as suggestions rather than orders.

The room grew loud again as people discussed which contracts each man wanted to tackle. Real squabbles were rare, even for the choicest gigs; everyone had good manners and their own unique skill set, preferences, and schedules. There was always somebody who couldn't work too far from home because his wife was pregnant, or needed to return in time for his nephew's wedding, or whatever the hell.

I tuned out most of my coworkers' chatter. I was still wrapping up my last assignment—a vulnerability assessment and risk mitigation for a major telecom company. And my bank account was plenty fat, so why drive myself nuts by taking on more work? Of course, I was curious about what Barton was holding so close to the vest, but he'd bring me in on it when he was ready.

After about twenty minutes of discussion, Barton interrupted. "All right, gentlemen, I get the picture. Keep yourselves safe this week, and I'll be in touch. You're all dismissed." But while everyone was leaving, Barton called out a brusque, "Maxwell."

I stopped in my tracks and faced the screen again.

"You did an excellent job these last two weeks. You're making quite a name for yourself among the FBI, specifically with Special Agent Donovan." Barton inclined his head. "He didn't ask me to pass on his comments, but I thought you'd like to know."

"I couldn't have done it without my teammates," I

replied. Such an answer was automatic. A military man always downplayed his contribution and never stole the spotlight. Plus, that assignment had been a cake walk compared to what I was used to. Just glorified babysitting.

"That may be true, Maxwell. But I recruited you for a reason. You were among my best and brightest, and so far, you've kept up the good work and haven't let me down."

Pride swelled in my chest. Before the ink had even dried on my discharge papers, Barton had personally asked me to come work for Redstone. It was a favor—and an honor—that I'd never forget.

"Thank you, sir." I corrected the old reflex. "I mean, Mr. Barton."

My boss's bushy eyebrows lifted slightly. I couldn't tell if he was amused or annoyed. "At ease, son. We've both been civilians for a long time now."

I nodded. *And I'm damn glad about that.* Quitting the Navy was the best decision I'd ever made; joining Redstone was the second best.

Outside the firing range, I hadn't shot my service weapon in nearly two years, and I didn't miss the action one bit. Training police officers and escorting at-risk executives was a welcome reprieve from messy SEAL business. Not to mention working whenever the hell I wanted to work. That freedom was definitely one of my favorite parts.

But even if I hadn't served under him, Jerry Barton wasn't the kind of man you called by his first name. He commanded attention and respect as easily as breathing. Just looking into those steel-gray eyes made my back straighten—with a little fear as well as admiration.

"There's something else." He paused and looked away from the camera. "I have a special assignment for you, and it's . . . personal to me."

"Of course. Name it."

"I will when the time is right. I'm still gathering a last bit of intel."

I nodded. "Understood."

I had no idea what kind of assignment could be personal to him. Maybe a vendetta against an old rival. Either way, he'd always been there for me, and so of course I'd help.

Seemingly satisfied with that, Barton ended the video call without saying good-bye. I turned off the projector and went back to my desk.

I was in for a long afternoon. While Redstone did provide physical security for important locations or at-risk VIPs, we outsourced whatever monitoring technology was involved—alarm systems, CCTV feeds, the works. I wasn't the guy running wires under people's desks. But I knew what needed to happen and who to call to coordinate it all. So today, I had phone calls to make and e-mails to follow up on from last week's assignments.

I'd only been working for a few minutes when Greyson ambled by. "What's up? We still on for the big game on Saturday?"

"Huh? Oh yeah, of course." I turned away from my computer. "I was actually thinking of inviting someone." Before he could ask, I added, "Yes, it's a woman."

Greyson's mouth twitched. "Daniella working this weekend?"

I nodded.

"You should definitely invite her, then. I can come check her out . . . see what's got you so interested."

Oh, for Christ's sake. I knew where Greyson was going with this. He wasn't exactly subtle about his disapproval of my lifestyle. Maybe disapproval was the wrong word; it was closer to unease, or even worry.

"Sure, why the hell not," I finally replied. "I'll text her right now." We had talked about catching a game sometime.

I pulled out my phone and typed a message: *Longhorns vs.*

Sooners on Sat. 3 p.m. my place. You in?

Greyson looked over my shoulder. "Really, dude? You're truly the master of romance."

"Since when do I care about that?" I hit the SEND button. "There. You get to meet Lacey this weekend. Now, fuck off and let me work."

With a smile, Greyson waved his middle finger at me and left for his own desk.

I settled in to wrangling subcontractors again. But as I composed e-mails and made calls, my mind still lingered on my phone, waiting for Lacey's reply.

Fortunately, I didn't have long to wait before my phone dinged.

LACEY: *I'd love to.*

• • •

When I got home, Daniella was lying on the couch in casual clothes, long limbs sprawled out comfortably.

I squinted at the book in her hands. The cover featured a young woman floating in outer space with a tentacled monster.

"You're reading that again?" I asked.

She let the book drop just enough to smile at me. "Yeah, why not? People keep interrupting me."

"Sorry," I said with a shrug. "You're working this weekend, right? I invited Lacey over to watch the game on Saturday."

"Duty calls. That should be fun, though." Daniella started to raise her book again, then paused. "So she's cool with our whole situation?"

"Yeah, I told her everything. Well, maybe not *everything*. But she got the gist of it."

Judging by Lacey's brief moment of shock on our first date, my love life was hard enough to wrap her head around without adding BDSM into the mix. And she didn't need to know all of our private details right now, anyway. If the moment called for an explanation later, I'd give her the short version.

"She said she was fine with it as long as I didn't expect any threesomes."

"I'm sure that broke your slutty heart into a million pieces," Daniella remarked dryly.

"Careful. You shouldn't insult the guy who holds the whip around here." I gave her a predatory grin.

She pretended to glare back, then laughed, and I chuckled too.

Daniella wasn't acting nosy, even though she was

probably curious about Lacey, and I was grateful for that. I knew she wouldn't read too much into my words.

Unlike certain other friends. *Damn Greyson . . .*

I liked Greyson a lot; he was the only other ex-SEAL at Redstone. I'd stayed close with our former team—West, Shaw, and Ryder—but Grey and I still worked together every day, so I was more in tune with him than the others.

But even though we always steered clear of each other's buried skeletons, his butting in about the women in my life could still get annoying. Greyson sometimes gave advice whether anyone wanted it or not, which made me feel like a fix-it project.

I started to untie my shoes, then paused, realizing I still needed to buy some food and liquor for that weekend's game. "I'm going back out to stock up for Saturday. Want me to grab you anything?"

Daniella hummed, considering for a minute. "I don't know . . . I'll go with you and see what looks good. I haven't had dinner yet." She rolled off the couch and onto her feet, dropping her book on the coffee table. "Let me put on some shoes."

At the liquor store, we grabbed our customary poison on autopilot—single-malt whiskey for me, wheat ale for Daniella—while debating what kind of beer Lacey might like.

Eventually we splurged on a couple of seasonal variety packs.

Then we walked across the street to the supermarket, where we picked up Daniella's favorite crappy sushi and the same huge frozen pizza we baked for every football game.

She pushed the shopping cart while I threw the items we liked inside. To onlookers, we probably seemed like the perfect picture of domestic bliss, just another happy couple grocery shopping together.

We had done all of this a thousand times before, and there was something comforting in the routine. It seemed like nothing could ever truly shake us up. My life with Daniella was next to perfect. *Wasn't it?*

I ignored the gnawing feeling that something wasn't quite right as Daniella and I made our way to the checkout conveyor.

Chapter Five

Lacey

Nolan's house was pale brick with dark wooden beams cutting across the exterior to form a masculine arch over the front porch. It was all one story, but appeared roomy nonetheless.

I trotted up the steps at five minutes to three carrying a big platter of smoked brisket, guacamole, and queso, with a bag of tortilla chips tucked under my arm. Nolan had insisted that I didn't need to bring anything, but my Southern hospitality demanded that I not show up empty-handed. And I *might* have been putting in a little extra effort because I figured I might meet Daniella today.

I was curious about this "other woman" in Nolan's life . . . his side piece. Until I realized that she got there first, and so *I* was actually the side piece.

With a strange feeling dancing in my stomach, I hesitated at his door. *Shit. What am I doing here?*

Nothing in my life could have prepared me for this moment. Yet here I was, standing at his front door, debating whether to knock.

Just stick to the plan.

Raising my knuckles to the door, I knocked twice.

Nolan opened it, looking as handsome as ever. His deep blue gaze latched onto mine. A warm shiver pulsed through me, bringing awareness once again to the intense attraction I felt toward him. He was dressed casually, in a white T-shirt that clung to his muscled torso, and loose jeans that still hinted at his powerful thighs.

Damn it. Eyes up, Lacey.

Without a word, Nolan allow his gaze to travel down my figure, taking in my casual, yet alluring ensemble, lingering over my breasts, my hips. It seemed he wasn't the only one being mentally undressed.

I'd paid extra attention when getting ready this morning. Blow-drying my hair so it fell in a thick, straight curtain down my back, slipping into my nicest jeans—dark washed and slim fit to hug the curves of my hips and round ass. My burgundy Oklahoma Sooners T-shirt was just a little too taut over my breasts. It had shrunk the first time I washed it, at the time, I'd gotten upset, but now it seemed that the almost-too-small top was a blessing in disguise.

I expected some wisecrack about wearing my team colors, but instead, Nolan leaned in for a brief hug.

"You look nice." He breathed the words barely an inch

from my ear, sending warmth rushing over my skin. It was the first time we'd had such close contact, and my body heated up accordingly.

We came inside to the kitchen. Nolan unloaded my armful of food onto the counter, next to a piping-hot oven pizza.

"What's all this?" he asked, looking down at the several containers.

"I thought we might want some game-day snacks." I bent down to pet the dog who had come out to sniff my feet. "And you must be Sutton."

He let out a grunt and wiggled his stubby tail. Nolan watched with approval as I gave the dog a few good scratches behind the ears.

"Is Daniella here?"

Just the woman's name sent hot jealousy spiraling through me. I'd never be okay with this. But it didn't matter. I had a plan. And I would stick to it come hell or high water. I just wanted to know what I was getting myself into.

"She's at work. Why, did you want to meet her?" he asked, his brows raised as if the idea of us meeting never crossed his mind.

I shrugged. "I just assumed. Since I was coming to your

place . . . and she lives here."

He shook his head.

As a knock sounded at the door, I was struck by the unmistakable feeling that things were about to get a whole lot more confusing.

Nolan opened the door and greeted a tall, muscular man who stood there. They did that thing guys do, a thump on the back and a one-armed hug.

"Lacey, this is Greyson," Nolan said.

Greyson smiled warmly at me, giving the impression that Nolan had supplied more information than that behind the scenes.

"It's good to meet you, Lacey," Greyson said, his rough voice neutral, but his eyes dancing with mischief.

"Former SEAL?" I asked him, ignoring the unspoken messages passing between the men.

"How'd you guess?" he asked.

I tipped my chin toward the trident tattoo peeking from his sleeve. I'd been around enough SEALs growing up to recognize it anywhere. More than that, I was no stranger to the world these men had lived through—the blood, sweat, and tears that tattoo represented. Most women probably threw themselves at such strong, confident men, even before they found out their past professions, but I only viewed them with a healthy dose of respect.

"Very good," Greyson said, clearly impressed.

Nolan, on the other hand, gave me a curious glance. "Drinks?" he asked.

"I thought we were just going to stand here staring at each other all afternoon," Greyson said, smiling warmly at me.

I chuckled and followed them back into the kitchen. A formal tour wasn't necessary. Nolan's home was an open floor plan. The living area held two warm brown leather couches and a flat-screen TV mounted above a stone fireplace. The kitchen was all rustic mahogany cabinets and smooth cream-colored granite. It suited him. Airy, comfortable, and non-pretentious.

He pointed down the hall and told me I'd find the restroom at the end. And the bedrooms too, I assumed.

"Let me grab our drinks real quick. Then I'll show you where I keep the good stuff," Nolan said, winking at me.

After he popped the cap off an imported beer and handed it to Greyson, he filled a crystal tumbler with ice, adding a measure of whiskey and just a splash of water.

Noticing my gaze, he held up the finished product and

remarked, "I'm a man of very singular tastes."

"Except when it comes to women," I said. *Shit. Did my filter just disappear?*

Greyson chuckled, sipping his beer.

"Can I make you something?" Nolan ignored my remark with barely a smirk on his full lips. "A margarita?" he asked, remembering my drink choice from last weekend.

He had a fully stocked bar with expensive liquor and cut crystal glasses for each type of drink. Martinis, red and white wines, highballs. Long-stemmed champagne glasses, which I guessed he rarely used.

"No, actually, I think a beer sounds good."

"Sure." He offered me a glass, but I opted to drink straight from the bottle, like Greyson was doing.

"So, Lacey, how did you end up hanging out with this dickhead?" Greyson grinned at me as he led the way back to the living room.

I chuckled and took the spot on the sofa next to Sutton. He grunted and looked up at me, then plopped his head down into my lap. Stroking Sutton's fuzzy head, I thought about how to answer. The truth certainly wouldn't do.

"We met at West's a couple weeks ago," was all I offered.

He grunted and turned his eyes to Nolan's. Again, a silent message passed between them.

They're obviously thinking about the same thing . . . but what?

As we sat and made small talk, I gathered that Greyson was just as damaged as Nolan, just as adept at hiding his true self. He stiffened whenever Nolan asked him about his personal life, answering only questions about their shared work or the game, before Nolan gave up entirely and focused on his drink. But Greyson was a riddle for another woman to solve.

Eventually the room fell silent as the game absorbed us, and I breathed a little sigh of relief. I drained half my beer and patted Sutton's head as it rested near my thigh.

"You know," Greyson remarked suddenly, "a woman who can make brisket this good . . . I think she's a keeper." He helped himself to another bite from the plate on his lap.

Nolan's eyes locked on mine again. A zing of heat ran through me. It was infuriating having no idea what he was possibly thinking. He'd invited me into his space, but so far he'd been quiet and impossible to read.

I couldn't help but wonder about his relationship with Daniella. Did he treat her like a girlfriend? I knew they had a complex relationship. But I couldn't help holding out hope that if he met someone he really connected with, then maybe

. . .

No. I couldn't let myself go there.

Even without her here, I felt her presence. The fresh-cut flowers on the dining table. The pumpkin-spice-scented hand soap at the kitchen sink. I doubted those were *his* touches. It felt weird being in her territory. The romance novel sitting on the kitchen island felt planted. I wondered if she'd purposefully left it there. Wanted me to see it. Wanted me to feel strange, filled with this tingly awareness that I was in *her* space.

"Can I steal you away?" he asked.

My heart pumped faster. "Sure," I said, rising from the couch to follow him toward the dining room as Greyson continued watching the game.

Nolan pulled open the sliding door that led to the patio out back, and I stepped through. Thankfully the blistering heat of the summer had faded into a pleasantly warm fall. The sun was just beginning its descent, leaving the sky to decide if mellow oranges or pretty pinks were to dominate that evening's view. Either way, the atmosphere seemed to glow with possibility.

"Is everything okay?" Nolan asked, joining me beside the wrought-iron railing. "You've been quiet today."

He had too, but I didn't point that out. "It's fine. I'm just a little out of my element."

And a thousand miles outside my comfort zone. Not only because of getting involved with Nolan, but living in a new state, away from all my family and friends. It was bound to throw a girl off a little. But it felt nice to have company, and something about his presence made me feel safe.

He placed a reassuring hand against my lower back. "I'm glad you came today," he said, his voice low.

I swallowed down a wave of nerves. "Me too." I meant every word of that, surprisingly.

I shifted my weight, looking out over his backyard. Neat lines from the lawnmower and a row of well-groomed hedges at the very back. *If only my life were that tidy . . .*

"So, how does all this work? Do you mind if I pry a little?" My cheeks heated slightly, knowing all the questions spinning in my mind. It was one thing to hear about it over drinks the other night; it was quite another to see it with my own eyes.

"Pry away." He chuckled softly, his hand slowly stroking up and down my spine.

Awareness zinged through me. It had been a long time since I'd felt a man's touch. Six months, to be exact.

Taking a deep breath in an effort to embolden myself, I released it slowly. "Do you bring other women home to your bed often? And how does . . . she feel about that?" I didn't want to say her name, but Nolan didn't hesitate.

"Daniella has lived here for two years, so yes, I have brought women home before. But other than the gorgeous woman standing in front of me, I'm not interested in seeing anyone else right now. If that's what you're getting at."

"Does she sleep in your bed?"

He shook his head. "No, it's me and Sutton in there, and since she can't stand him, it's never even been on the table." His hand stilled, giving me time to process his words. "And whenever I . . . play with Daniella, it's in her bedroom, not mine."

"Play?" The question sprang from my lips without thought. *Damn lack of filter again.*

Nolan shifted beside me, dropping his hand from where he touched me. I immediately felt a sense of loss.

"Daniella's interests are somewhat . . . dark."

A shiver of real concern ran through me. I didn't know this man, not really. What if he was into things I couldn't possibly tolerate?

"Does she bring men home too?" I asked next. Although

curiosity gnawed at me, I wasn't sure if I was ready to hear the extent of his kink just yet.

His expression tightened. "No. And not because I'm against it—that'd be pretty fucking hypocritical of me—but because she's not interested in other men. She's always been a one-man kind of woman." Then he studied me. "What else is going on inside that pretty head of yours?"

I glanced away for a moment, embarrassed that he'd seen through me so easily. "I admit, I'm curious about those . . . interests you mentioned." *Yours more than hers.*

"I see. Well, without going into too much detail, Daniella is a submissive."

My belly tightened into a knot as my hunch about Nolan's dominant side came into clearer view. Taking a deep breath, I reminded myself why I came here. I wasn't allowed to fall for this handsome man anyhow, so what did it matter if his sexual tastes were a little darker than mine? I got the bodyguard I needed, while Nolan and Daniella fed each other's need for kink. Everybody won. So why was my stomach twisted into a knot?

"H-how did you get this way?" I cringed when I realized how it sounded. Like I thought he was damaged goods. Then again, maybe he was.

But he didn't even raise an eyebrow at my question.

"After a demanding career as a SEAL . . ." He let out a deep sigh, gazing out at the yard. "My goals are much simpler now. I just want to enjoy life one day at a time, take pleasure where I find it."

I simply nodded. He didn't elaborate, but he didn't need to. I knew he had seen too much, done too much, probably experienced losing teammates he fought beside. Battle could mess a man up. At the very least, it changed them. And in Nolan's case, it made him harder and closed him off to the hearts-and-flowers kind of love I hoped to find someday. He was surviving, but in his own way.

"Now my work isn't quite so intense. I'm a consultant for a private security firm called Redstone. And while it can be dangerous, it's not nearly as life-and-death as my previous world."

Looking down, I gave a nod of acknowledgment. I already knew all about Redstone, but it was good to hear him say that his life had improved.

Chuckling softly, he returned his hand to my lower back. "Come on. What else did you want to know about Daniella?"

Was I being that obvious? "How did she end up living here with you?"

"I knew her through a mutual acquaintance, and after

breaking up with her ex, she needed somewhere to live. I had a spare room—three, actually—and I offered her a place to stay. Rent-free. No strings. And she said yes."

"That was awfully nice of you." I blinked at him in wide-eyed astonishment. It wasn't something many people would do.

"Trust me, I'm very far from being a white knight." His voice dropped lower and his hand moved slowly along my spine again. "Our relationship sort of evolved from there."

He didn't continue, leaving me to guess at the specifics their BDSM relationship might involve.

"What happened to her?" Something must have gone down, if she'd needed Nolan's help so suddenly.

"Let's just say she was pretty banged up when I got her." He went still for several moments, as if he was lost in a somber memory. "She's safe now," he added.

It was the kind of heroism I'd expect from a Navy SEAL. Rescue. Relief. I wondered if he'd banged down the door to her ex's place and made him suffer. A rush of warmth spread through me at the thought.

Nolan glanced at me. "Would it make you uncomfortable to be in my bed, knowing she was just down the hall?"

I thought about it for a moment. "Yes, it probably would a little," I finally admitted.

He nodded once, as if he was expecting my answer. "I don't want to talk about Daniella anymore."

"You don't?" I murmured, lost in the deep unending blue of his eyes. They were stormy and filled with tension.

Slowly, he shook his head. Bringing one hand up to cup my cheek, he stroked his thumb over my skin. "I think you're sexy as hell," he growled. "And Grey was right, that brisket was fucking incredible."

I smiled and leaned into his touch as his gaze lowered to my mouth. Running my tongue tentatively across my bottom lip, I felt the air around us change, grow more heated.

"I need to know what you taste like," he murmured.

I blinked up at him, my eyes still searching his. There were so many things I was unsure about, but the electricity buzzing between us wasn't one of them.

Leaning forward, Nolan brought his lips to mine and waited, as if to give me a chance to decide. His warm breath ghosted over my mouth.

Accepting his invitation, I stood on tiptoe and touched my lips to his. With one hand still stroking my jaw, his other came to settle against my hip, his thumb running along the bare skin at the waistband of my jeans. He pulled my body close, until I felt the hard ridge of him against my belly. He felt massive. My lips parted in a silent gasp and he stroked his tongue against mine.

Our mouths seemed made to fit together. And the skillful way he moved his tongue provoked thoughts of how else he could use that tongue. My panties grew wet and my breathing ragged as we kissed.

My hands wandered, running over his firm biceps and down the front of his shirt, where rounded pecs waited invitingly.

Sex rolled off of him in waves. No, not just sex. *Fucking.* I was sure that being intimate with Nolan would be unlike any other experience I'd had. And that excited the hell out of me. Maybe there was something about its forbidden nature that appealed to me too. He'd already been claimed by another woman, and I hated that I saw that as a challenge— but damn, I did. And I wanted to rise to the occasion.

"Sweet Jesus, woman," he murmured, breaking away from my lips.

I couldn't disagree. Everything about that kiss felt right. Backgrounds ceased to matter. Messy entanglements forgotten. When I was kissing Nolan, nothing mattered except getting even closer. *More,* my body begged. For such a strong and intense man, I hadn't counted on the sweet way he was with me, the deep, yet soft kisses and tender touches. He made me feel safe, and to me, there was no better feeling in the world.

"Just keep an open mind," he said, tucking a stray lock of hair behind my ear.

With my lips tingling and the taste of whiskey on my tongue, I gave him a small nod. "I will."

"Come on. Let's go catch the rest of the game."

"Okay." I nodded again.

Nolan brushed his lips against mine one last time. "We'll take this at whatever pace you need, okay?"

The sincerity in his eyes, his voice, made it impossible to disagree with him.

• • •

After getting home from Nolan's, my lonely little apartment felt too quiet, so I called my younger sister just to hear her voice. Brynn was away at college but we had remained close, talking on the phone or texting a couple of times a week. At least, until I'd lit out to Texas.

"Lacey, where are you?" Brynn cried before I could even say hello. "Everything that's happened . . . Troy . . ." She didn't finish her thought, and she didn't have to.

"I know. I'm safe. And for once in my life, I might even find something that makes me happy." Brynn knew all too well that my life so far had revolved around making other people happy.

"You're not going to do anything crazy, are you?"

I couldn't help the chuckle that pushed past my lips. I thought of Nolan and all the reasons why I shouldn't pursue him. And there were many.

"Define crazy." I pushed my hair off my face and flopped down on the couch. Quitting my job on a whim and not telling my sister I was leaving until I was already gone? Yeah, it was a touch insane.

"Damn it, Lacey. We were raised by a drill sergeant of a father, and you never once stepped out of line. Then shit went down with Troy, and now you're gone. What am I supposed to think?"

Letting out a heavy sigh, I considered telling Brynn exactly where I was and what I was up to. Then I quickly decided against it. *The less she knows, the better off she'll be.*

"I've met someone." I didn't mean to blurt it, but there it was, hanging in the silence between us.

"Ah. So that's what's been taking up all your time." Her tone turned light, playfully mocking.

Regret churned inside me. Part of me wanted to confide in my sister, you know, for when all of this went tits-up and I needed someone to fall back on. But what would I say? *Oh yes, he's tall, dark, handsome, and he has a live-in lover.* No, that wouldn't fly.

"Well, that was . . . fast," Brynn said.

As soon as the words left her mouth, I felt them like a sting across my cheek.

"Sorry," she added after a long pause. "That was probably harsh."

"Don't worry about it," I said, forcing a lighthearted tone. "I have to go. We'll talk soon." I tapped END on my phone's screen.

Somehow I doubted Brynn would understand my new life in Texas, my job at the animal shelter, and certainly not my motivation for a relationship with a sexy-as-sin ex-SEAL. But how could I expect anyone else to understand it when I didn't understand myself.

Rising from the couch, I tossed my phone onto the mountain of purple silk throw pillows I'd collected. Lavender. Violet. Lilac. Plum.

I felt restless and edgy, but didn't know what to do about it.

Sometimes I let myself think about Troy. Allowed my mind to drift back to happier times. The way he'd play with my hair and tell me I was his girl. Our Friday-night tradition that went without saying. Baking homemade pizzas that my unreliable oven always burned on the edges, then scrambling onto the couch, because whoever got the remote first controlled which movie we'd watch.

We had a quiet and comfortable relationship until things went and turned insane. And now here I was, running from a past I didn't even understand.

Then I remembered something my father told me a long time ago. *If it scares you, run straight toward it.*

I should trust my instincts right now, should let myself pursue the one thing that felt good in my life at the moment. It was already hard to imagine calling off this thing I'd started with Nolan.

As I stood at the front window with my hands on my hips, my mind replayed this afternoon. Nolan's stolen kisses. The presence of Daniella looming in the background. His friend, Greyson, who watched us as if we were his own personal soap opera, just waiting for the drama to unfold.

Was I insane? It seemed that way. But I couldn't deny my attraction to Nolan. The big, broad man inspired feelings deep down inside that I'd never expected. Of course, he was handsome, six foot four, muscled from head to toe . . . but it was more than that. There was a depth to him, something that I could *feel* when he looked into my eyes. Like he was just waiting for someone to understand him, to peel back his layers and accept the man he was. And I wanted to be the one to explore his depths.

After my ordeal with Troy, the last thing I was looking for was another messy entanglement. I was here to keep my head down, start fresh, and find a path where I'd be safe and happy. And instead, after being here for less than a week, my life was already turning complicated.

I sighed as my gaze wandered over toward the parking lot. Something prickled against my spine, making my posture straighten as awareness zinged inside me.

That white car . . . it was familiar. It had been parked in the same spot all day. I'd seen it when I walked down to Nolan's for the game more than four hours ago. There had been a man sitting in the driver's seat then, which didn't seem all that strange at the time, but he was still there. Watching. *Waiting.*

The room chilled and feelings of panic slammed into me. Stumbling back from the window, I grabbed my phone, double-checked the locks on the front door, and retreated to my bedroom.

Locked behind my bedroom door, I fired off a text to Nolan. My growing feelings aside, this was about staying alive. I needed him, much more than he needed me. My plan was going to work. *It had to.*

LACEY: Would you like to come over for dinner tomorrow night?

Chapter Six

Nolan

The next afternoon, I was watching TV with Sutton draped over my lap like a drooling sandbag. Neither of us paid any real attention to the evening news, but both of us were enjoying our lazy Sunday. I'd learned not to take life's small pleasures for granted.

When my phone dinged on the end table, I reached over, jostling Sutton and prompting a peeved grunt. It was a text from Lacey: *Can we do dinner at 7:30 instead of 6? Sorry for short notice; shitstorm at work today.*

Wondering if she meant that literally, given that she worked at an animal shelter, I texted her back: *I can come over in five minutes and lend a hand.*

Her apartment was just a short drive down the road. Food definitely wasn't what I craved most right now, but I decided not to say that. At least, not via text. Some things were better said in person, and even better murmured into a woman's ear.

Her reply came almost immediately: *That's okay. Please don't go out of your way.*

I rolled my eyes, knowing how these Southern rituals of

polite refusal worked. I typed out the next step in the dance: *No worries. I want to help out.*

As I hit SEND, I realized that I actually meant it. Cooking wasn't an interest of mine, but making dinner with Lacey actually sounded fun. Although I'd probably have to hold a gun to her head to get her to accept my offer.

About five minutes later, she responded: *Well, if you really insist . . .*

"Huh. That was easy," I said to Sutton. She still hadn't been able to bring herself to say yes, but I'd expected a full-blown etiquette arms race.

The bulldog just stared back at me mournfully.

"Sorry, buddy."

She probably wouldn't mind if I brought him along—she seemed to love the little gasbag almost as much as I did, and said gasbag loved table scraps. But I wanted some uninterrupted time with Lacey tonight. So I nudged Sutton to the floor, ignoring his grumbles of protest, and coaxed him into my bedroom with a treat.

Then I made the short trip over to her apartment complex and knocked on the door. She answered in cutoff jean shorts and a forest-green T-shirt with a howling wolf on it. Her feet were bare, showing pearly pink toenails, and her long brown hair was corralled in a loose, messy braid. Except for her bright eyes, she looked like she'd just rolled out of bed—and it made me want to roll her right back in.

"Hey, there." Her smile was a little sheepish. "I told you not to come yet . . . it's going to be super boring. The pot roast has to cook for three hours."

She must have just come home from work, washed off what little makeup she wore, and put on her house clothes. Had she wanted to change into a nicer outfit for me? To open the door looking prim and polished, with dinner already on the table? That shyness was kind of cute. But she didn't need to try to impress me. She had my full and undivided attention without even trying.

I shook my head, smiling back. "I don't mind hanging out for a while. I've got nothing better to do today." And I could think of worse ways to spend an afternoon. Lacey looked adorable, her hair mussed and her cheeks flushed in the Texas heat.

"In that case," Lacey's smile turned crooked, "I'll have to put you to work."

I followed her into the kitchen. Her place was small, but tidy, with cute feminine touches. She slid a chef's knife from her knife block, handed it to me, and pulled a small mesh bag of white onions out of the fridge.

"Can you cut all these into big chunks for me?"

"Sure, I'd be happy to."

I pulled the cutting board close and started on the pile of onions.

As I chopped onions and peeled garlic cloves, she washed and quartered the carrots, potatoes, and celery. This atmosphere felt different from when Daniella and I did household chores together. Preparing ingredients with Lacey felt warmer somehow. Something simmered between us, just beneath the surface.

I'd never understood the appeal of domesticity. It always sounded soul-crushingly boring. But in this moment, I could maybe see why my married coworkers talked so fondly about coming home. Seeing their wives' familiar, affectionate smiles after a long day, giving them a hello kiss, helping them keep house.

When I finished my share of the vegetables, I noticed Lacey still working on hers. And there were tears streaming down her cheeks. *What the hell?*

"Did the onions get to you?"

She shook her head, quickly wiping her eyes. "I'm so sorry. I thought I'd be fine once I got home."

Remembering her text from earlier, I placed a hand on

her shoulder. "Tough day at work?"

She smiled sadly. "Something like that."

"You can talk to me."

I wasn't even sure why I said it; what had started between us as instant physical attraction and carefree fun was quickly turning into something more serious. Normally that would be enough to send me running, but right now, all I wanted was comfort her. Hold her tight. Make her pain go away.

"They put down Charlie today," she said haltingly as a fresh wave of tears filled her eyes.

"Who's Charlie?"

"An old basset hound. He was so sweet . . . I loved him. B-but he was in kidney failure, and they didn't want him to suffer anymore." She buried her face in her hands as quiet sobs shook her shoulders.

I stood awkwardly for a moment. If there was one thing I was clueless about, it was crying women. Daniella wasn't the emotional type, I had no sisters, and my mom was one tough cookie. The one and only time I'd seen her cry was at my dad's funeral.

Then realization struck. That's exactly what this was, but without the casket or flowers. Lacey had lost someone she cared about today. Before I knew it, I had pulled her to my chest, shushing her cries and telling her all about the last person I'd lost: my old teammate, Marcus Sutton, who my new best friend was named after.

As I spoke, the memories rushed back.

Watching my mom become a shadow of her former self after losing her other half hadn't put me on the fast track to commitment. The spunky, book-club attending, wine-swilling, foul-mouthed woman I'd grown up loving because she was so different from my friends' soccer moms had been replaced by a hollowed-out shell who wandered the house with a vacant look in her eyes.

Mom tended to her garden. Watched the evening news. Occasionally brought over a pan of lasagna for Daniella and me to share. Just went through the motions of life. She put on a brave face, but that kind of loss wasn't something that healed. And while I loved her as much as ever, I hated the situation we were in.

Lacey's sobs subsided as she listened to my story. I wasn't even sure why I was telling her all this. I just needed to fill the silence, needed to occupy her with something other than her own sorrow.

"Shortly after I lost my dad, I flew back to Fallujah. I'd been there only a few days when a car bomb was detonated near our post, sending shrapnel flying in every direction."

Lacey pulled back from her spot at my chest to listen. She could tell that this was the clincher of my story, the freshest and deepest wound.

"Marcus Sutton had a new wife at home, a house with a white picket fence, and way too much on the line. I held his head in my lap and felt his blood oozing through my uniform pants." My voice shook, and I took a deep breath to compose myself.

What I didn't tell Lacey was that that was it for me. As the light faded in Sutton's eyes, a single tear streamed down my cheek. All I could think of was Marcus's bride waiting at home, just like Mom still waited for Dad. Her heart might have kept on beating, but she'd become a ghost right along with him. I couldn't even imagine the heartbreak that Finley Sutton was in for. I knew that torment would last for years to come. So right then and there I'd vowed *fuck love*. It got you nowhere but broken. *No fucking thank you.*

Lacey stepped back and wiped her eyes a final time. "I'm sorry for breaking down like that. I know losing a dog is nothing like losing a best friend, and especially in such a tragic way." Her eyes met mine, and I could see that she felt my pain.

"Please don't apologize. I'm glad I'm here with you tonight."

Letting out a sigh, she nodded. "Me too."

"We'll have a good meal, and you can tell me more about Charlie if you want," I offered.

She smiled sadly. "No, really, I'm okay. It's just going to be weird walking in tomorrow and seeing his bed empty. I think this is just hitting me hard because I'm homesick. I'm feeling extra emotional."

"Trust me, I understand loss more than anyone. You can talk to me about it if it helps."

"I'll keep that in mind."

Deciding that the best thing to do was to keep us occupied, I found the butter, greased the Dutch oven standing on the stove, and switched on the heat so it would be ready to sauté. I turned around to grab the onions and saw Lacey watching me.

"What?" I grinned as I poured the onions into the pot. They smoked with a satisfying hiss as they touched the hot butter. "Surprised to see a man cook?"

She blinked, her cheeks turning a little pink. Maybe she'd been staring at me for a different reason. Was she surprised I had a soft side under my thick, war-battered exterior?

"N-not really," she replied. "I know the military makes you do mess duty and learn some home-ec skills."

Oh yeah. I remembered that she'd recognized Greyson's trident tattoo last night. Usually women either had no idea what it meant or instantly dropped their panties.

"How do you know so much about the Navy, anyway? You have a relative who served?"

Lacey tensed. "Yeah, a . . . relative."

The odd tone to her voice signaled it was clearly a sensitive topic for her. I should probably back off; no point in digging into something she didn't want to discuss. Especially not with the day she'd had.

To change the subject, I asked, "So where did *you* learn to cook? Your mom teach you?" I stood back so she could add her brimming bowl of vegetables to the pot.

She shook her head. "No, it was our housekeeper." She pointed to the steaming pot. "Those only need to sear for a minute. Put them back in the bowl when you see brown."

"A housekeeper, huh? Was your family well off, then?" I stirred the vegetables in quick, efficient figure-eights.

She forced a little laugh. Her somber expression bothered me more than it should have. "Not really. Dad could have cooked, but he was always working, and Mom . . .

wasn't around."

Wow, I'm a complete tool. That was twice now I'd stumbled into a sore spot. Usually I was pretty smooth with women, if I did say so myself. My bedpost certainly had enough notches in it.

"Sorry." I sighed. "That was none of my business."

She shook her head, and her comforting smile was genuine. "It's not a big deal. It happened a long time ago."

Lacey didn't seem to care how far I'd stuffed my foot into my mouth. And even though I was apparently way off my game today, I realized that I was still having a good time. Being here with her felt so comfortable.

She pulled the raw chuck roast out of the fridge and started sprinkling it with salt, pepper, and spices. Watching her was strangely captivating. But the vegetables were dangerously close to done, so I contented myself with an occasional glance at Lacey's delicate hands, massaging the seasonings into the glistening roast.

After the meat was also seared and set aside, she pulled out a carton of beef broth and a bottle of red Burgundy to deglaze the pot. "I was going to have a glass of this and watch a movie while I waited for dinner." Raising the bottle, she smiled—invitingly—at me. "What do you think?"

I grinned back. Now, this was a plan I could get behind.

We transferred all the ingredients back into the pot, slid it into the hot oven, and went to the couch with two glasses of red wine. I sat down barely an inch away from Lacey.

"Are you sure you're doing okay?"

She took a sip of her wine and nodded. "Yes, I'm really glad you're here."

"Agreed. You shouldn't be alone right now. Did you have fun last night?"

"You mean the game, or . . . ?" She leaned a little closer.

I reached out to stroke her cheek and she closed her eyes, sighing almost silently. I set my glass on the coffee table and pressed a chaste kiss to her mouth.

She pulled away slightly, but only to set her glass aside too. "I did have fun," she said softly, brushing her lips against mine.

There was nothing chaste about my next kiss, and she met me with equal hunger. I knew I should take my time, but fuck, I didn't want to.

I wrapped my arms around her, flattening our bodies together, pushing her down to squirm under me. She seemed so small like this. I wanted to gather her up, to protect her and pleasure her, and keep her for myself.

It took me a moment to recognize that fleeting spark of

possessiveness for what it was. I hadn't felt that way about a woman for a very long time. Usually I was content to enjoy whoever I was with, and then get the hell out of there when we were done.

Holding Lacey this close, I could feel her breathing hitch slightly whenever I nibbled her lower lip or stroked my tongue around hers. I mapped her mouth for every spot that made her knees tighten around my waist.

Daniella and I never kissed, and I was quickly realizing how much I loved it. It was strangely hot and sweet at the same time. Everything else in my life melted away, leaving only Lacey—her soft curves, soft skin, soft lips, soft sighs.

But I couldn't ignore the pressure building fast in my groin. I rocked into her, grinding my hard bulge between her legs. She squeaked into my mouth.

"You like this?" I knew damn well she did—her hips had stuttered up to meet mine. But I wanted to hear her say it out loud.

"Y-yeah," Lacey said softly.

I rewarded her with another quick, hard kiss. She tried to kiss back, only for me to pull just out of reach. "Can I touch you?" I asked.

Her sapphire eyes had already gone dark with desire. As soon as she nodded, I pounced.

I lavished her neck with long, sucking kisses as my hands roamed her body, squeezing her plush tits over her shirt—

Oh God, no bra under there; she'd been bare this whole time.

She gave a quiet moan and I took that as encouragement to push up her shirt. Eager to make her feel good, I moved my mouth lower to lick and gently bite her soft pink nipples. Spurred on by the sexy little sounds she made, I pushed myself between her legs, letting her feel how much she excited me.

Lacey groaned again.

I was torn between wanting to make her feel good and not wanting to push her too far, too fast. A quick fuck on her couch probably wasn't what she'd had in mind when she invited me over tonight. And something about her made me want to take my time, savor her in a way I'd never done with a woman before.

I bent forward to kiss her again, long and slow, while massaging her gorgeous breasts. I couldn't keep my hands off them. Such a beautiful set of tits deserved to be worshiped, touched, kissed, licked, *bitten*. The desire to mark her skin flared inside me, and I only barely beat it back.

Lacey rocked her pelvis up to grind against me, and a

tortured growl clawed up my throat.

"Careful, sweetheart," I warned.

I was on my best behavior at the moment, but if she kept rubbing her warm pussy up against me, I wouldn't be for long. The thought of stripping her shorts away and pounding into her tight, hot cunt almost edged out every ounce of my good sense.

Somehow, some way, I reined myself in, letting her set the pace. We remained clothed, kissing and groping and grinding until I thought my cock was going to burst. But our leisurely make-out session was strangely satisfying on its own. More than enough—at least, for now.

How could such a tame act be so much fun? Maybe I'd been missing out on a good thing for all these years. Or maybe kissing only felt this good with Lacey.

Something to ponder for another time.

We cuddled and kissed in front of a movie she picked, some feel-good comedy that left me free to focus on her warm softness against my side until the oven timer rang. Then we served ourselves the delicious-smelling feast. At the first tender bite, Lacey's coo of pleasure made me lean across the table and kiss her yet again.

Despite all the scars we'd bared—or maybe because of them—tonight had been nothing short of perfect. But my past had taught me not to trust so easily. As happy as I felt right then, I couldn't shake the unsettling feeling that things were too good to be true.

Chapter Seven

Lacey

When my boss insisted on happy hour, I couldn't exactly refuse. I'd wanted to go home, get out of my slobber-soaked jeans and T-shirt, and take a hot bath, but I figured one drink couldn't hurt.

Jamie was a recent divorcée, and while she was friendly and outgoing, she was also a bit like a cougar on the prowl. A *rabid* cougar.

Soon we were sitting at West's bar, the same place I'd met Nolan the week before, drinking jumbo-sized margaritas. It was ladies' night, which meant two cocktails for the price of one.

Crap . . . so much for just grabbing one quick drink. I could only hope my boss wouldn't drown her romantic sorrows too hard.

Jamie set her frosty glass down on the table, looking forlorn. "The next man I'll even consider dating will need to have a steady job and no mommy issues."

I made a sympathetic noise that she could interpret however she wanted. Her standards weren't exactly high, but hey, who was I to judge?

"And maybe not so selfish in bed," she added, lifting her glass in a toast. "What about you?" She hiccupped. "Special man in your life?"

I shook my head. "No, not really." I found myself feeling protective of Nolan, and I didn't want to share the intimate details of our . . . whatever it was.

I winced at the memory of how emotional I'd gotten the other night. I couldn't believe I'd broken down like that. Sobbed on his shoulder over a dog I'd known for all of three weeks. But Nolan had been so sweet and tender about the whole thing. Holding me as I cried, telling me his own story about the friend he'd lost. I was quickly starting to feel more for him than I ever dreamed possible.

Nolan's love life was a hot mess, but he was also handsome and strong and honorable. I couldn't walk away now, not even if I wanted to.

Soon one drink with Jamie turned into two, then three. When a round of shots was set before us, compliments of a couple of guys at the bar, Jamie squealed and handed one to me. As I sucked on the little lime wedge, I realized my head was starting to spin. There was no way I'd be driving home tonight. When I passed by the bar on my way to the restroom, I stopped at the counter, leaning over to ask the bartender if he would call cabs for my friend and me. He nodded and picked up his phone.

A few minutes later, the bartender wandered over and introduced himself as the owner, West. He was a tall, muscled linebacker of a man. Handsome, but a little scary.

When he announced that our cabs were here, Jamie stood and grabbed her purse, and I followed suit, thanking him. Outside, she climbed inside the yellow minivan and waved, saying she'd see me at work. As the van drove away, I realized that West must have assumed we'd share the cab. Meaning that I'd just missed my ride.

"Damn it." I looked around the all-but-deserted parking lot, wondering what I was going to do now. Surely there was more than one cab in this entire town.

Then I froze. There, at the back corner of the lot, was a white sedan with its interior dome light on. I couldn't be sure it was the same car from last week, but cold dread still crept through me, raising the hairs on the back of my neck and making me step back.

No way was I waiting out here. I'd just have to go back inside and ask West for another cab.

"Come on. I'm driving you home."

The familiar voice surprised me, and I spun around to see Nolan approaching through an opening between the parked cars. Relief flooded through me, weakening my knees.

"How did you . . . ?"

"My buddy West called me. He recognized you as the woman I was with the other night. Said you asked for a cab."

"And he asked you instead?"

Nolan nodded. "I'm taking you home." His firm tone left little room for negotiation. He was definitely a man who always got what he wanted.

Through my heavy buzz, I took a moment to look at him. He wore faded jeans and a white T-shirt. I wondered if he'd been at home, in for the night. Maybe hanging out with Daniella. And he'd left the warm comfort of home to head out into the night for me. A tingle of appreciation spread through me at the thought.

"You don't have to do that," I said instead.

"I'm quite aware. Come on, get in the truck." Nolan led the way and helped me inside. He glanced over at me as he started the engine. "How much did you have to drink?"

"It was ladies' night," was all I said. I thought I heard him chuckle softly, but couldn't be sure.

He didn't say anything else as he drove. The tires crunched over the gravel road and the radio played quietly in the background. Within minutes, we pulled into my building's parking lot. I let myself out of the truck and started toward my apartment. But when I reached the stairs, Nolan's hand caught my elbow.

"I can manage," I said, both warmed at his concern and embarrassed that I needed it.

"I know that," he said, but didn't remove his hand.

I guess chivalry isn't dead.

When we arrived at my door, he stopped. I'd expected him to walk me there and then leave, his sense of obligation fulfilled, but that wasn't the case.

"Can I help you inside?" he asked instead, his low voice sending tingles of heat rushing along my skin.

This time, I said, "Yes."

Unlocking the door, I slipped inside. I flipped on the hall light and tossed my purse and keys on the table. Then I just stood there, wondering what I was supposed to do next. I wasn't good at these games, hadn't had a man rush to my rescue before.

"Do you have to work in the morning?" he asked.

I nodded. It was only a little after ten, but I had a hunch I'd feel the tequila in the morning.

Nolan headed into the kitchen and poured me a glass of cold water from the pitcher I kept in the fridge. "Come on.

Let's get you ready for bed."

I led the way to my bedroom. I was about to argue, to tell him I was too old to be tucked in, but the careful way he held my hand and helped me into my room spoke louder than anything else. He was a natural guardian, and right now, he was going to see to it that I was okay.

In my darkened room, Nolan stood directly before me, the soft moonlight painting his face in shadows. He was beautiful. A strong jaw dusted in dark stubble, full lips, and dark, soulful eyes.

I felt his fingers at the hem of my shirt. He lifted it over my head, dropping it on the floor beside us. His fingers went to work on the button to my jeans, and then he was pushing them down my hips. Next came my bra, which he unsnapped and slid off my shoulders.

His watchful gaze wasn't lustful; it wasn't sexual. It was protective. And I could sense it all the way to the tips of my toes. Standing there in just my panties, I felt my body hum to life, blood pumping south.

"Don't you want to stay?" I gingerly touched his belt buckle.

"You're drunk," he said. His voice was blunt, and I sensed his control was hanging by a thin thread. A thread I wanted to tug on and unravel.

"So? We could still mess around."

Working his bottom lip between his teeth, he let out a hiss when I brushed my hand lower, appreciating the bulge I felt. "Not tonight," he bit out.

His rejection stung, and I couldn't help the first thought that popped into my head. "Oh, so it's Daniella's turn tonight."

"Not tonight," he repeated.

Unwavering in my desire, I pushed my fingers into the sides of my panties and dragged them down my legs before stepping out of them. Now I was completely nude before him. My nipples puckered in the cool evening air.

He didn't miss a thing, his gaze moving from mine down to my breasts. He lowered his head and kissed one pebbled bud. Just the barest teasing touch.

"Not. Tonight," he repeated once more, his warm breath ghosting over my nipple.

In that moment, I would have done anything he asked. But instead of letting things go further, my perfect gentleman adjusted the bulge of his erection, then stuffed his hands into his pockets. "Do you have something you sleep in?"

I nodded. "Just a T-shirt."

He retrieved one from my dresser and held it out so I could shove my arms in and get it over my head. One quick kiss on the lips, and he was headed toward the front door.

"Lock up behind me, okay? There are crazies out there."

"I know." *Boy, do I know.*

• • •

Several days later I stared down at my bed, trying to decide between the jeans and a light gray sweater, or the red sundress and boots. I wanted to look casual, but with a certain measure of sex appeal too.

This morning Nolan had texted me, letting me know that he had two tickets to the Cowboys game, and his friend had to cancel at the last minute. AT&T Stadium was a venue I'd grown up watching on TV with my dad; the chance to go there in person wasn't something I could pass up. Neither was spending more time with Nolan.

Opting for comfortable, I slipped into the worn denim and the soft, lightweight sweater. After adding my boots and checking my butt in the mirror, I felt oddly satisfied. My curves filled out my jeans a little more than I'd like, but I knew the effect I had on Nolan. I'd felt the evidence of his arousal, hot and hard and needy against my belly. A rush of warmth washed over my skin, flushing my cheeks at the memory. He'd held himself back, but maybe that was only because I'd been drunk.

Shit. It's time to go.

I grabbed my small purse, double-checking that I had the essentials—my ID, some cash, cell phone, a little tin of mints, and a tube of tinted lip balm. I wasn't much for frills, but fresh breath and kissable lips were high on my priority list today. Because holy hell, the man could kiss.

Closing my eyes for a second, I remembered the way his mouth felt on mine, how dominating and sensual he was when he moved. The way his tongue stroked mine, the feel of his steely erection pressing between my legs, so close to where I wanted it . . .

Damn. Just thinking about him made me ache. I shook off the dirty thoughts and left, locking the door behind me.

I trotted down the stairs and found Nolan waiting for me just where he said he'd be. Right next to his big black pickup truck.

His gaze swung over to watch me approach, and I couldn't help treating him to an extra swish of my hips. He took note, his mouth quirking up into a lopsided smirk, his eyes dancing with mischief.

"You ready?" he asked once I was close.

"Absolutely." I treated him to a warm smile, thankful to have someone to spend time with in this new town. He opened the passenger door of his truck, which looked like it had just been washed. The sleek finish gleamed in the sunlight.

Without a clue about how to climb up into the beast of a truck, I placed one foot tentatively on the running board, then hesitated.

"Up you go," he said from behind me.

I could feel his eyes on my butt as his hands came to rest at my waist. Effortlessly, he lifted me onto the seat. The muscles lurking under his shirt were more than just pretty to look at, it seemed.

"Thank you," I murmured, finding my voice.

When Nolan got in beside me and started the truck, country music played low in the background. I had to smile. This quiet, comfortable life he'd built for himself after retiring from one of the world's most demanding jobs was enviable. On the outside, at least, he seemed to have it made.

Leaning close and placing one hand on my cheek, he murmured, "I need to taste these lips again."

So it wasn't just me affected by those kisses.

His mouth covered mine and I opened, letting him

stroke my tongue softly but so surely that a small, murmured groan clawed up my throat.

"Fuck, sweetheart." He grunted out the words, yanking away like I'd burned him. His voice a little strained, he said, "We'd better go."

I agreed, my "yes" sounding just as breathless. My heart was still pounding wildly. *Or else we'll end up back inside, humping like bunnies.*

As Nolan drove, his hand found my knee and rested there casually. It was crazy how that one small touch both heated my blood and made me feel safe. We made small talk, and he pointed out some landmarks as we drove to the stadium.

When we arrived, we parked in the large lot and walked quite a distance toward the stadium. We climbed the stairs almost as long to reach our seats. Center field, twelfth row up. They were excellent, with a clear view of the field. But when we took our seats, Nolan's hand once again rested on my knee, making it hard to concentrate on anything else.

"You doing okay?" he asked, sending me a sideways glance.

"Fine." I cleared my throat. *Get it together, Lace. He's as hot as a July day in Texas, but that's no reason to clam up.*

He waved over a vendor and pulled a stack of bills out of

his pocket. "What would you like?" he asked me.

"Whatever you're having is fine." He'd already treated me to the game, and I didn't want to be picky.

He ordered us two beers and stadium dogs, tipping the vendor well. The man's eyes widened and he thanked Nolan profusely.

Nolan was a man of few words, but it was in these quiet moments that I learned the most about him. Not only was he a tough, kick-ass ex-SEAL, but he was kind, generous, and warmhearted. The combination was enough to kick-start my libido and dampen my panties without even adding in his rugged good looks.

Being around him was easy, and once I had a cold beer and a warm hot dog in my hands, I began to relax a little. I took a big bite of my food and settled into my seat.

"So, what made you want to become a SEAL?" I asked, expecting that it had been a lifelong dream from the time he was just a little boy with a toy gun strapped to his waist and a fort in his backyard.

Nolan looked down at the field, his expression stark, his dark eyes blank. "I grew up a rancher's kid, and I wanted to see more of the world than the flat prairie inside our four fence posts."

I nodded along, afraid I'd struck a chord that would sour the playful mood. "Fair enough."

"But it turned out that was pretty fucking selfish of me. My dad had a massive heart attack in the field one day while he was working, and with no one there to help, no one to call 911 . . ."

He let out a deep sigh and his eyes shifted away, taking several moments before he continued. "I still ask myself if I'd been there that day, maybe he'd still be around. Maybe my mom wouldn't look at me with those blank, haunted eyes, like she was wondering the exact same thing."

I reached over and silently placed my hand on his knee, hoping the touch had the same calming effect it had had on me earlier.

"My mom sold off all the land he loved so much. I don't think she liked the thought that the land was ultimately what took him from her."

Something tugged inside my chest. I wished like hell I could fix this for him, but deep down, I knew nothing ever would. Sometimes our greatest scars are the ones we don't wear for the world to see. They're buried inside our hearts.

I gave him the only comfort I could. "I know your dad would be very proud of you. If he'd known what a successful and courageous man you've become, he never would have wanted you to stay home. Just think of all the things you couldn't fulfill if you didn't leave."

Nolan smiled at me, but his thoughts still seemed faraway. "Maybe. Enough about that, though. I meant today to be fun."

I squeezed his thigh in silent understanding. "Another beer?" I waved down the vendor again. "My treat this time."

"Did I tell you that you look beautiful today?" he asked, leaning across the space to place his lips at my neck.

My throat tightening, I shook my head. "Not yet anyway."

"Because you look fucking stunning," he whispered against my skin.

Maybe sex was his way of dealing with the demons of his past. A distraction, a release. *Is that what his arrangement with Daniella is about? Or is he just too much for one woman to handle?* A rush of warmth settled in my chest at the thought.

With our second drinks in hand, the earlier lighthearted mood returned. Soon we were cheering and trash-talking the athletes on the field, enjoying each other's company and the crisp fall day.

• • •

Arriving back at my place after the game, Nolan parked under the awning that stretched alongside the building. We sat quietly and watched the sun sink low in the sky. The atmosphere around us took on a hazy glow as day slowly transitioned into night. The warm cab of his truck was scented lightly with the dark notes of his cologne, swamping the space with sexual undertones.

I couldn't remember ever having more fun. But when I turned to tell him so, the deep, penetrating look in his eyes stole my breath. It was almost like I could read his every thought—and they were searing. His gaze was filled with a dark, primal urge that called to something inside me.

"I'm running from something." The words sprang from my mouth without warning. And once they were out—hanging between us in the silent cab of the truck—my heart started to pound.

"Care to tell me what, sweetheart?"

I shook my head. "I can't tell you. I'm sorry."

He was quiet for a moment. Then he reached over and placed his hand on my knee, giving it a squeeze. "Nothing's going to get you."

"No? Why not?" Hope blossomed in my chest, and I hung on to his every word like it was a lifeline.

"Because they'd have to get through me first. And that

ain't fucking happening on my watch."

My heart slammed against my chest and my breathing shallowed. Those were the best words on the planet; everything I'd longed to hear.

But I knew something he didn't. Something that would make him put me on the first plane back home without even a good-bye. My secret had seemed too big and important to tell at the time, but now, I wished I'd just come clean from the beginning. Because I knew the truth would have to come out at some point, and by then, it would be a huge, ugly divide between us. An insurmountable lie of omission.

But Nolan didn't press me, didn't take me by the shoulders and demand answers like I expected. And his blind trust stung more than if he'd yelled and screamed in my face and demanded I come clean.

I waited for him to say something more, but he didn't. Which was good, because I didn't have the answers he needed.

Suddenly, he leaned over and seized my mouth in a possessive kiss. A whimper escaped me and my fingers dug into his shoulders. The kiss turned deep and molten, our tongues dueling for control. I wasn't about to back down from this big, powerful man who held the promise of my entire future in his hands.

He hauled me across the front seat's center console to straddle his lap. The massive bulge in his jeans was unmistakable. The man was hung, and apparently his cock was hungry. For me. I wanted to feel it in my hand, in my mouth . . .

"You taste so fucking good." He grunted, pushing up his erection to brush against my clit.

I groaned as his lips moved down the column of my throat and my hips circled just once, needing to feel the hard ridge of him. Pleasure and warmth ripped through me. *Shit.* I was quickly becoming addicted to this man.

Suddenly his hands were everywhere—my face, my neck, gripping my waist, caressing the underside of my breasts. Need unfurled inside me. Dying to feel his hands on my skin, I let out a frustrated groan.

"You still want to take this slow?" he asked, his mouth lifting in a smirk.

"Yes. I mean no," I muttered.

A dark chuckle rumbled in his chest and I hated myself for that slip-up. But something inside me did need to take this slow. Despite my darker motivations, I didn't think I could give myself to a man who was in another relationship.

"Tell me if I get too rough," he breathed, his teeth lightly grazing my neck.

Those words sent twin bolts of hot fear and desire through me. His hands moved with grace, yet total control. He gripped both of my wrists in one hand while he devoured my neck, his teeth grazing my collarbone. He was possessive in all the best ways.

With my hands pinned, I was immobile, only able to kiss him back and rub wantonly against him.

His free hand slipped up my side until he reached my chest. My breasts felt so full and achy, as if I could come from his touches there alone.

Nolan's fingertips grazed my nipple, and even through my bra, the contact was enough to perk it right up. His hand cupped and massaged, and I lost myself in the pleasure.

His kisses were deep and penetrating. I felt them all the way down in my belly, my panties becoming wetter with each flick of his hot tongue. Blood thundering in my ears, I wanted time to stand still so this moment would never have to end.

Raw need stabbed at me. The desire to feel his body joined with mine, to feel him thrust deep inside me was nearly overwhelming. A ragged sob broke from my throat, and Nolan pulled away.

"You like my hands on you, sweetheart?"

"Yes." I panted out my response, unable to find the words to express just how very much I liked them. Rough. Calloused. Strong, yet so decisive in their movements.

He resumed his sensual assault, kissing and caressing me until I was a sopping-wet puddle of need.

My body bucked up and down on his, my clit begging for friction against his thick denim-covered cock. Feeling how virile and masculine he was made me forget about every silly worry I'd had before. I wanted the dark, rough ride he promised—as hard as he could dish it out.

Despite my best efforts, his military-inspired discipline shone through. He kissed hard, nipping at my lips, yet didn't try to press me to take things further. But the rumble in his chest signaled he wasn't immune to my movements against him.

A rough sound pushed past his lips, somewhere between a grunt and a gasp.

I wanted to hear him make that sound again, and as often as possible. My movements grew frantic and, impossibly, I felt myself building toward climax. Even fully clothed, that didn't stop him from nursing an orgasm from my body.

God, how good would it feel if we were naked?

"Let go, sweetheart," he said softly against my neck.

Before I had a chance to ask him what he meant, he cupped both my breasts, rolling my nipples between his thumbs and fingers, and I bucked wildly against him.

"Come for me," he commanded again. "I want to watch those gorgeous sapphire eyes glaze over with lust."

My body, having gotten the permission I didn't know it needed, started the quick ascent to orgasm. My tender flesh throbbed, my clit pulsing in time with my rapid heartbeat.

I could feel the heat of him through my jeans and rocked back and forth, my climax right there, so close . . .

"I'd rather be inside that pretty cunt of yours, but ride it, baby, take what you need," Nolan whispered in my ear.

His filthy encouragement did me in. I fell over the edge, my body trembling as a powerful orgasm crashed through me, making me cry out. Blinding pleasure sprinted through my veins and drowned out everything around us.

As aftershocks pulsed through my body, I buried my face in his neck, my heart racing. I should have been embarrassed about riding him like a mechanical bull in his truck, but my lust had driven out any shame.

Realizing I was still planted in his lap, I climbed back over into the passenger seat of the truck, discreetly checking

Nolan's lap to make sure I hadn't left a wet spot there. *God, that'd be embarrassing.* He wasn't wet, but he was still rock hard, the entire front of his jeans bulging.

Unable to tear my gaze away from his erection, I asked, "Don't you want me to . . . ?"

"No. You don't have to." His gaze was laser-focused on me, genuine concern in his eyes. "Hey, are you okay?"

"Of course. I'm fine," I said. Something clicked in my brain. A sour voice whispered, *Maybe he hasn't pushed you for sex because he's getting it from someone else.* The realization stung hot and bitter in the center of my chest.

"I should go," I said, drawing my purse into my lap.

Thinking about Daniella shouldn't bother me so much. I shouldn't care why Nolan didn't want me to get him off. But my throat was still knotted with disappointment.

"Hey. Just breathe." He used two fingers under my chin to bring my gaze to his. "I can't promise you romance, and I sure as fuck can't promise you forever, but I can offer you this. Now. And I promise everything I'm feeling for you is real."

I nodded, still dizzy from the power of my earlier release, and utterly confused about where this was all heading. I was starting to feel something real for him too.

And that was very, very dangerous.

Concepts like right and wrong, single or attached seemed murky at best.

I wanted him—plain and simple. But would he still want me when he learned the truth?

"I'm going to be out of town for a couple of nights," he said finally. "But I'd like to hang out again when I get back."

I nodded. "Okay. I'll talk to you soon." I stumbled from his truck, still in a daze, wondering where this path could possibly lead me.

Chapter Eight

I've been watching you. I know your routines, your habits. You come home from work, dead tired, and sometimes make yourself a cocktail while you turn on the TV—not to watch it, just for the background noise. Then you take a long shower that fills the bathroom with steam.

When you emerge from the shower, you're more clear-headed and calm. But you always worry . . . I know it. I see the stress etched into your brow.

I know you wonder. About me. About the future. You do a damn good job pushing those worries away; I'll give you that. But not quite good enough.

I know your secrets, your desires, and the skeletons you'd prefer remained hidden. The closer I get, the more you pull away.

It's strange how connected we are, yet you have no idea. No fucking clue about everything I've been through.

I'm almost done waiting. Almost ready to take back what's mine.

Chapter Nine

Nolan

It was late afternoon when I pulled my black pickup truck back into my parking space. These last few days had been long and tiring. Under Redstone's name, I'd helped the Fort Worth police department investigate a puzzling spike in gang activity. Apparently, an Oklahoma City drug ring had imploded about a month ago, and some of its members had fled across state lines.

But I didn't give a shit about that anymore. I'd fulfilled my contract, pocketed my check, and now I was back on my home turf. And there was only one person I wanted to see right now.

For the entire drive back into town, the memory of Lacey planted on my lap in the cab of my truck had tortured me through every mile. The sounds she'd made as she rode me were burned into my brain. Helpless cries and shaky whimpers that went straight to my dick, made my balls draw up just thinking about it. *Damn.* I couldn't get her out of my head. Yet something about the whole situation felt *off* somehow. I couldn't shake the unmistakable feeling that I needed to proceed with caution. Figure out my next move.

I turned off the truck and grabbed my phone to send a text to Daniella, letting her know I was back in town. I didn't get a response right away, not that I expected to. Having been gone the last several days, I was unaware of her work schedule. Exiting the truck, I walked straight to Lacey's apartment and knocked on her door.

When she opened it, she grinned and threw her arms around me. "You're back."

Her open affection was different from what I was used to, but my whole body relaxed at her touch. My hand settled against her lower spine, returning the warm physical contact.

I had taken that out-of-town gig in the hope that some distance would clear my head. Help put this woman situation into perspective. But with Lacey in my arms, I suddenly couldn't remember what I'd been confused about.

"Did everything go okay?" she asked.

I shrugged. "Yeah, just some drug ring from Oklahoma City. The police are zeroing in on them, and they needed some extra support."

She looked frightened for a moment, and I smoothed a thumb along the worry crease on her brow. "Hey, it's okay. We'll get the bad guys. We always do."

She nodded, and her features slowly relaxed as she took a steady breath. I wasn't sure if her extreme reaction was because this particular job hit close to home, or maybe just because it originated in her hometown. Either way, something prickled in the back of my head.

"I'm glad you're back home safe," she said finally.

I nodded. "How are you? How was work? Feeling better about Charlie?" Lacey didn't really need me to check up on her, but it gave me an excuse to visit.

She nodded, looking only a little sad. "Yeah. Putting him down was the right decision. I just needed some time to accept it."

"Well, I'm glad you're doing okay. You want to get some dinner later?"

"I just ate, so I won't be hungry for a while. But . . ." Her hands flattened against my back, fingers rubbing gently. "Wow, you're hard as a rock."

"Thanks." I chuckled.

She flushed a little. "Not hard like that. I meant you're tense." A hint of mischief lingered in her smile. "Can I give you a massage?"

I bent my head for a chaste, but lingering kiss. "Is this an excuse to get me shirtless on your bed?"

"Of course," she murmured against my lips. Then she took my hand, lacing our fingers together, and led me

111 • Kendall Ryan

through the apartment to her bedroom.

I leisurely unbuttoned my shirt, watching Lacey watch me. She was so beautiful when she looked at me softly like that. Her eyes told me all the things she didn't say. That she viewed me as a protector. That she trusted me. Wanted to believe in me. Even though I'd all but admitted my wicked ways to her, she saw past my sinful nature—and she still wanted me. It was a good feeling. Being accepted for who I was, not forced into some mold of who she wanted me to be.

It was different from the way Daniella looked at me. Of course she trusted me; you didn't let a man tie you up and fuck you unless there was a hell of a lot of trust there. But Lacey was looking for something on a whole other scale. I could feel it. A man to care for her, guide her . . . and I'd be damned if I didn't want to be that man.

Once I was free of my shirt, Lacey's eyes darkened and lit up with lustful fire at the same time. I lay facedown on her bed, head on my arms. She straddled my lower back and started rubbing my shoulders, digging her fingers into the stiff muscles with surprising strength. I groaned aloud at the mix of pleasure and relief.

Hazily, I tried to remember the last time I'd gotten a massage, and came up blank. But I found that I liked the intimacy—lying half-naked, pinned down, just letting a beautiful woman tend to me. I could get used to this.

It was strange how such innocent touches could be so erotic. She gradually worked her way down my back, unknotting my tension inch by inch. Her thighs squeezed my hips for balance as she leaned forward. Her round ass fit perfectly into the dip of my lower back, and I could feel the growing heat between her legs.

My cock responded accordingly. I shifted my hips, trying to get more comfortable, but my erection was trapped under my belly, and squirming on the bed just made it worse.

Lacey might have taught me to enjoy taking sex slowly, but there was only so much temptation a man could resist. I wanted her, and I knew she wanted me. Deciding to move things along, I twisted and took her down with me, rolling us both onto our sides.

"What are you—" she started. Right before my mouth met hers in a firm, hungry kiss.

Pressing herself closer, she hooked one leg over mine, and I rocked my hips into her pelvis to let her feel what she'd done to me.

Lacey groaned. "I take it you liked the massage."

"What gave me away?" I asked, breathing hard against her neck.

"A certain wayward southern appendage." She ground into me again, her hips moving against mine.

I almost chuckled. Almost called her out for being too prissy to say the word *cock* . . . until her hand slid down to my jeans to unbutton me.

"Maybe he needs some attention too," she rasped against my throat.

I hadn't come here for this and wouldn't have pressed her, but I also wasn't going to turn her away. We would take things at whatever pace she wanted.

Tugging down the zipper to her shorts, I was desperate to touch her and bring her pleasure. It was as if every time we were together was a completely new experience. Fingers and mouths and heartbeats thumping together. And hormones raging at an all-time high.

I pushed my hand inside her shorts, fumbling when she reached down to grip my denim-covered erection. *Christ.*

My fingers soon found what they were looking for. She gasped as I rubbed in slow circles through her panties. Even with the cotton barrier, I could feel the firm bud of her swollen clit. I sucked in a breath when she tightened her fist, kneading my hard cock.

"Together," was all she said. But I understood.

Only a little impatiently, I waited until she had unzipped my jeans before slipping my fingers under her panties. I gave a soft groan at the feel of her hot, slick folds.

"God, baby, you're so wet already."

"All for you," she murmured huskily. "Touch me, please."

I obeyed in a heartbeat, echoing her moan when she pulled my cock free and started stroking up and down with whisper-soft strokes.

This was nothing like sex with Daniella. In our sessions, I always held myself at arm's length, preserving the image of the stern, in-control Dom that she needed. My body might bind and strike and fuck, but because everything was on my terms, my heart stayed safely locked away.

But right now, even though I still had my pants on—and Lacey hadn't gotten undressed at all—I had never felt so naked before. Staring into her eyes like this, breathing her breath, I couldn't hide anything about myself.

More importantly, I realized I didn't want to hide. I wanted her to see the real me, because I knew she would accept it. She saw all my flaws and weaknesses, all my regrets and nightmares, without so much as a flinch. Instead she smiled at them, as if to say *I wouldn't have you any other way. This is what makes you who you are.* And I let myself be swept along in the ocean of her eyes.

Carefully I slipped two fingers inside her, desperate to give her pleasure, to lose control with her. Her body gripped me tightly and she let out a soft moan.

I wanted to know Lacey in the same way she knew me. To get rid of everything between us—no fear, no pride, just skin on skin. When she shivered, my cock throbbed with her excitement, and her pussy squeezed my fingers.

Our arousal echoed back and forth as if our nerves were linked. Her pleasure matched mine, rising higher and hotter with every moment. Our arms and legs tightened around each other in anticipation. Moaning aloud, we dissolved together.

Long after our pleasure had faded, we still held each other tightly, legs entwined. The setting sun had painted the bedroom walls in gold. I rested my chin against Lacey's forehead and inhaled the lavender scent of her hair. Her breath fanned over my neck. Our chests touched in a gentle rhythm, falling apart, rising together.

I wanted to stay like this forever. And that was exactly why I had to leave.

• • •

Back at home, I poured kibble into Sutton's dish, trying to figure out what the hell just happened as the bulldog gobbled his dinner with slobbering crunches.

I'd never felt such a deep connection to a woman before. Like the outside world had just melted away, leaving me and Lacey to become our own universe. Like I could see my own future in her eyes.

This afternoon with her had been sweet, gentle, incredibly hot . . . and utterly terrifying. I'd done some pretty filthy things in bed, even before Daniella, but I'd never been so vulnerable, let alone welcomed that vulnerability.

I went to the couch, Sutton lumbering after me. Seeing Lacey had felt amazing, but once I was away from her, all my vague restlessness rushed right back. I needed to stare at the ceiling and think for a while. Or maybe I was already overthinking. Maybe what I really needed right now was some mindless TV.

But just as I sat down, the front door's lock clicked. Daniella swept in with a heavy sigh.

"Ugh, work was fucking awful today." She untied her tennis shoes and tossed them into the entry closet. "Two nurses called in sick, and some jack-off yelled at me because he had to wait for two hours in the ER. Dude, the candlestick up your ass ain't going nowhere. Let's deal with the gunshot wounds and heart attacks first."

"Wow, that sucks," I replied in a monotone.

If Daniella noticed my distracted state, she didn't care. Her tired smile turned hungry as she walked around the couch. "It did really suck. Fortunately, I know a great way to unwind," she purred.

She leaned over to rub my shoulders, pressing the back of my head into her cleavage. Her hair tickled my neck, and I irritably brushed it aside like a mosquito.

Even an idiot could tell what Daniella was waiting for. She wanted me to get up, grab her arm, drag her into her bedroom, tie her up, spank her ass raw, and fuck her until she screamed. But the thought just didn't appeal right now. Even though I could feel her nipples through her shirt, piercings and all, my cock resolutely stayed limp.

"I don't know," I finally said. *I don't know anything.*

All of a sudden, I felt very tired. I'd taken that Oklahoma City job to clear my head, but half a week away from these two women hadn't helped at all. Thoughts of Lacey had kept distracting me. In the middle of reviewing witness depositions or analyzing CCTV footage, I'd catch myself wondering what she was doing. Wishing I could spend time with her—not necessarily having sex, but definitely not in a "just friends" way, either. And then that weird moment in bed tonight . . . lying on our sides facing each other, staring into her hooded eyes as we came apart together.

"You don't know? What does that mean?" Daniella's hands paused on my shoulders. "Are you saying you're not up for it?"

Shaking my head, I shrugged. "Sorry—"

"No, it's okay," she said, cutting me off as she stepped back. "How did your mission go?"

"I don't do 'missions' anymore. But it went fine—no real hiccups." Sutton bumped his head into my leg, grumbling for attention, and I reached down to scratch behind his ears.

When I didn't elaborate, Daniella nodded in resigned acknowledgment. "Well, that's always good to hear." She paused for a moment before asking, "You're still taking me to the Nurses' Ball, right? It's this Thursday."

"Of course . . . I remember. My tux is at the cleaner's, but I'll be ready." I always followed through on my commitments. *Always.*

She smiled, and I felt myself relax a bit. Seeing that smile was important to me. I'd nursed her back to health after a massive broken heart.

"Don't freak out, but I had an idea," I started. It was

something that had been stewing in the back of my mind for the last few weeks, and I wanted to hear what she thought.

"What?" She raised one brow in curiosity.

"What if I took you back to the club?"

After her ex dumped her, Daniella had stopped visiting the local BDSM club they'd once frequented together. That disappearing act had hurt a lot of her friendships. It pissed me off to watch Daniella isolate herself like this. Her ex had been the asshole here, but she was the one being punished. Even two years later, she was still too afraid of running into him to go where she damn well pleased.

She frowned, taking a step back. "Why? Because you're trading me in for Lacey?"

"What? No, of course not. It's because you're stronger now. I thought you might be ready to take that kind of step again."

"I have no interest in that, Nolan. Being here with you is as close to perfect as I've ever had."

With just those few simple words, she tugged on my heart. I really was her savior. "It was just a suggestion."

Her hands came to rest on my hair. "I have everything I need right here. Are you sure you don't want to . . ."

"Not tonight." The words felt like acid on my tongue.

Seriously, what the fuck is wrong with me?

She stepped back again and stretched hard, squeaking as her back popped. "Then I think I'm going to take a nap before dinner. Holler if you need anything." She headed to her bedroom—obviously planning to spend some quality time with her vibrator.

But then she stopped in her tracks. "Nolan?"

"Yeah?" I turned my head to see her staring at me from halfway down the hall.

"Could she ever . . . change what we have?"

Her voice was so sad, her eyes so dark. Sympathy squeezed hard inside me.

"No. Never," I heard myself say. "You know I'm never going to settle down with a wife and kids." I smiled at her to tell her it was the absolute truth. "That's not me, babe."

She grinned back. "I know that. You're like a wild horse. Roaming free, not meant to be tied down."

"Exactly."

"You're always going to want a sub on the side."

I didn't say anything else. What *could* a man say to that? I just watched Daniella head to her bedroom, until I heard the door click shut behind her.

Looking back down at Sutton, I cupped the dog's jowls and stared into his saggy brown eyes.

What the fuck was going on here? This wasn't the first time I'd turned down Daniella, but before, it had always been for some concrete reason. I was nursing a hangover, had to get up early the next day, whatever.

I still wasn't sure why I didn't want Daniella right now. Why my thoughts kept returning to Lacey, like iron filings drawn by a magnet. Why I felt a strange gnawing that I couldn't put my finger on—a nagging sense of unreality.

As a Navy SEAL, I'd suffered through blood, sweat, and tears. I'd escaped from six years of hell and built the life I'd always wanted. Easy pleasures. Good friends, good sex, good whiskey. A laid-back, well-paying job where I could come home to my own bed every night.

Right now, though, all those hard-earned rewards were starting to feel insubstantial. But what more did I want out of life? What more *was* there? The only thing that quieted this strange dissatisfaction was . . . thinking about Lacey.

I let go of Sutton's squishy face. I couldn't figure out what I wanted or what to do about it. And even though Daniella had said everything was cool, I'd heard the edge of frustration in her voice. She'd really been hoping for some relief tonight. She downplayed her disappointment, trying not to make it my problem, because she wasn't the manipulative type—but I could tell she wasn't happy with me. And I couldn't help but feel kind of shitty about disappointing her.

It was as though she sensed that, as my feelings for Lacey grew, my connection to her was fading—and that made Daniella want to cling to me even harder. I didn't blame her. The idea that Lacey could represent the end of life as we knew it . . . that terrified me too. Daniella and I had been each other's security blanket for so long, and change was scary, even when it might lead to something good.

I stood up. Enough of this bullshit. I needed to get off my ass and do something productive, and if that something was just to consume a fuck of a lot of whiskey, so be it. I needed advice too, and Daniella wasn't the right person to ask. I also wanted to get out of the house to avoid the guilt trip I was sure was coming later.

I pulled out my phone and texted Greyson: *You home yet? Want to get a drink at West's?*

When Greyson replied, *Sure, I'm not doing anything tonight*, I clipped Sutton's leash onto his collar and went out. We should take advantage of the warm, breezy weather while it lasted, before the evenings got chilly.

I walked the few blocks to West's, found a free table on

the back patio, and tied Sutton to its umbrella pole. I ordered whiskey on the rocks for me and a bowl of water, which I set on the ground for Sutton. Greyson arrived a few minutes later, grunting a low "hey," and ordered a beer.

After a few minutes of sipping our drinks in silence, I put down my tumbler. "I was hoping I could ask you something."

"Really? And here I was, thinking we were just out on a nice date." Greyson rested his chin on his fist. "I guess that means I'm paying for my own drinks tonight."

"Screw you," I replied without heat. "It's about Lacey."

Greyson sat back and raised his glass to his lips again, nodding in a silent *go on*.

I stared into my amber drink. "She's all I think about, man. I want to see her all the time, make her smile. It's making me wonder ..." I let myself trail off because I sounded like a Grade-A pussy.

"Wonder what?"

I threw up one hand in exasperation. "That's it, man. I don't fucking know. Wonder about my life. Whether I'm going in the right direction."

"So, what you're saying is, you like her."

"No shit, Sherlock. I generally don't fuck women I hate."

Actually, I hadn't fucked Lacey at all. We hadn't gone that far yet. But somehow, I felt more from one of Lacey's touches than I'd let myself feel in a very long time.

"I meant that things are starting to get real." Greyson raised his eyebrows for emphasis.

"That . . . no. What? No way." I huffed a little laugh that didn't sound convincing, even to me. "You know me, right? The guy who's never had a girlfriend for longer than a few months?"

"Yeah, I do know you. And that's how I can tell what's going on here." Greyson flashed a smug grin that I immediately wanted to slap right off his face. *The dipshit.* "I've seen the way you look at her. And Daniella says you've been spending a lot of time together."

I rolled my eyes. "You've been gossiping with my roommate? Are you a woman?"

"Shut up and listen. It's obvious to everyone but you that you have feelings for Lacey."

"It's not—"

"Have you even wanted to fuck another woman since you started dating her?"

Giving up, I rubbed my forehead. Grey didn't need to know how close to the truth he was. I'd been putting off

Daniella's advances for the past couple of weeks now, ever since Lacey had arrived in my life.

Despite what I already shared with Daniella, I couldn't deny that I needed something more. Something more *primitive*. The kind of intimacy shared between two willing lovers. No ropes. No toys. Just two bodies fucking wildly. Moving together.

Was it selfish? Probably.

"Okay. Just for the sake of argument, let's say you're right. What should I do?"

"Sorry, man. I'm just here to shine a light on your shit. I can't tell you how to handle it."

"Well, what would you do?"

Greyson's smirk slipped. "We're not talking about me here," he said, his voice a little icy. Then he quickly joked, "I'd fuck it up like always. But this is you. Whole different ball game."

"Obviously. But can't you just—" I stopped, at a loss for words again. I was getting tired of this confusion. "Give me something to go on here?"

"Hmm, I dunno." Greyson picked up his glass again and took a sip. "I guess the main question is, do you want to get serious with Lacey?"

"But what does 'serious' even mean?" I snorted. "I'm not getting married, if that's what—"

"Did I fucking say that? Christ." Greyson gave me a look. "There's plenty of room between 'no strings attached' and 'buried together.' Maybe you meet her parents. Maybe she moves in with you. Maybe you just set up a standing date every Friday night." Greyson waved to indicate a wide world of commitment possibilities. "Just pick a step beyond where you are now and try imagining it. Do you like the picture you get? Then walk toward that future."

I considered it as I polished off my last drops of whiskey. As unhelpful as Greyson's plan sounded—and as much as I didn't want to hear it—that idea was still better than anything I'd come up with.

Finally, I sighed. "Okay. I'll think about it."

"Glad I could help." Greyson gave me a satisfied nod. "And you should talk to Daniella later. She'll probably have an opinion too."

Oh shit. Daniella . . . and Laccy, at the same time. That hadn't occurred to me. I knew how to juggle multiple casual partners, but having both a submissive and a steady girlfriend was a totally different matter. That wasn't something I'd ever counted on. This was all supposed to be in the name of good fun, but once real feelings came into play . . .

Greyson was right. I had to figure out what I wanted before shit got really messy.

I'd always prided myself on my ability to develop multiple contingency plans; it was a damn necessity in my line of work. Yet I had no fucking clue what I was doing with Lacey.

Daniella made sense. I could provide her what she needed without ever risking myself, without ever getting in so deep that my heart could be ripped out. I never wanted to feel that sense of soul-crushing loss ever again.

So the question was . . . play it safe, or take a risk?

Chapter Ten

Nolan

"I'll get us another drink," Lacey called from the kitchen. "Whiskey?"

We'd met at West's for a drink after work, and then drinks turned into dinner, and now we were here, back at her place.

"Sure," I replied, but something else had caught my attention. She had a record player on a desk in the hall.

I crossed the room and twisted the little knob on the side and soft music rose to life, something soulful and unexpected. A woman's voice floated over deep notes of bass guitar.

It wasn't familiar, and wasn't anything like the music my parents had played at night when they thought I was in bed. I'd sneak down the stairs, sit on the bottom step, and watch them. Mom's eyes would close as she rested her cheek on Dad's shoulder, a soft smile playing on her lips. They looked happy. Calm and at peace.

Damn. I felt a little pang in my chest; I missed those tender moments more than I'd care to admit.

Lacey came back, carrying a glass of white wine for herself and a whiskey on the rocks for me.

"Come here." I offered her my hand. She set the drinks down on the coffee table and placed her palm in mine.

"What are you . . . ?" she began to ask, before a grin took hold of her lips and her question disappeared into the dimly lit room.

I placed my other hand against her trim waist. She sucked in her breath when I pulled her in nice and close. Maybe I was a little drunk. Maybe I was feeling sentimental. But if we were doing this, we might as well do it right.

"Do you know how to waltz?" I asked.

She smiled at me. "Not even a little. Show me?"

"Gladly."

We swayed to the music, her chest brushing mine as we moved. Her pounding heart felt like hummingbird wings. One song faded into the next, and still I didn't want to let her go. She smelled like sweet rain and peppermint, and I wanted more.

After several minutes, the record stopped, the player continuing to spin with soft crackles in the background.

"Where did you learn to do that?" she asked.

I led her over to the couch, where we sat down and each

took a sip of our drinks.

"My mother taught me when I was young. I didn't think I even remembered."

She smiled at me again. "You're a complicated man, Nolan Maxwell."

"And here I thought I was simple."

She was silent for several minutes. Then she set down her wine and turned to me. "For the right girl, could you ever . . . wouldn't you want . . . ?"

"No, sweetheart." I stroked her hair away from her face and met her eyes so she could see the solemn truth in my words. "And not because I can't do it. I *won't*." I'd seen what happens, felt the crushing sting of loss, and it wasn't something I cared to repeat. "Besides, I have a responsibility to Daniella."

"Right. *Daniella*." She looked down at her hands.

The name rolled bitterly off Lacey's tongue, but I didn't chastise her. There were some things she couldn't even begin to understand, and I doubted I could do them justice if I tried to explain them.

"Did you have fun tonight?" I asked, hoping to draw her out of her somber thoughts.

Her chin lifted, her eyes meeting mine again. "Yes."

"Come here."

Cradling her jaw in my hands, I brought her mouth to mine. Her mouth opened obediently and I stroked my tongue against hers, the pressure immediately building in my groin. These were the things I understood. My body's response to hers, the need to see her come undone with pleasure.

I pulled her over to straddle my lap. She immediately circled her hips to brush against my firm cock, moaning when she felt how hard I was already. The mood changed in an instant, hot need coursing between us.

"You are so fucking hot, I don't want to stop." I echoed her groan, pushing my hips up to meet hers.

"I don't want you to."

The longing in her voice spurred me on. I rose to my feet with Lacey's legs locked around my waist. Her mouth went to my neck while I carried her to her bedroom. The little licks and nips of her teeth went straight to my dick.

Inside her room, I laid her down on the bed and pulled her shirt off over her head. Her breasts were perfection; the generous cleavage spilling over the cups of her lacy bra begged to be kissed and sucked. But I had something more pressing in mind.

As slowly as I could, I kissed my way down her body, stopping just before her waistband. "I want to taste you, sweetheart."

She swallowed, watching me, her eyes wide.

I knew she wanted to take things slow. That was fine. We could have plenty of fun without ever breaking out the condoms. And judging from the hot spark in her eyes, she knew exactly what I was about to do. She was ready and more than willing.

I unbuttoned her jeans and pulled them down her shapely legs. As I brushed my fingertip over the front of her cream-colored satin panties, Lacey drew a shuddering breath. She was soaked.

"These panties are ruined, angel."

My tone was harsh, my erect dick strangling away all coherent thought. I wanted on top of her, inside her, but I wouldn't do anything she wasn't begging for. I took my time stripping the wet scrap of fabric away, appreciating the view. Shaved bare with delicate lips concealing her pink inner petals, she had a pretty cunt, and I wanted my mouth all over it. All over her.

Breathing in through my nose, I kissed her bare pussy, letting my tongue slip down to taste between her folds. She sucked in a sharp gasp. *Fucking hell, she tastes sweet.*

I took my time tasting her—I'd never tire of her unique

flavor, tangy and sweet all at once. Her thighs tensed under my hands with every gentle lick, just barely enough to drive her crazy without getting her anywhere. I teased her until her clit stood out from its sheath, a swollen pearl begging for my touch.

"Nolan . . ." Her voice was almost a whimper.

With gentle flicks of my tongue, I teased her clit until it was engorged, and her entire body was quivering, begging for release.

"This pussy gets nice and swollen for me," I said between licks, and she squirmed beneath me, making a helpless whimper.

Done making her wait, I dived in for the main course, parting her with my thumbs so I could suck her clit into my mouth. She had to clap a hand over her mouth to stifle her cries. But she couldn't hold back when I slipped one finger into her pussy. She fit so snug and hot around me that my cock ached. I could feel her inner walls trembling under the onslaught of sensation.

Slowly sinking my finger in and out, I teased her opening with another, getting ready to slip the second one in alongside the first. But she moaned my name and her pussy clamped around my finger in wave after wave of pleasure, her thighs twitching around my head as she bucked into my face.

Damn, that was fast. "Did that feel good?"

She nodded slowly, still looking a little dazed. My male pride swelled—along with a certain other part of my anatomy. Sex with Lacey was turning out to be one wild ride. Her body was so responsive, as if every touch was a brand-new sensation.

Then I suddenly wondered if it *was* brand-new. Lacey did act a bit sheltered sometimes. But maybe her previous lovers had just been incompetent.

"Has a man ever gone down on you before?"

If she was indeed a virgin, I should have been approaching sex a little differently this whole time. But shit, better late than never.

Lacey blinked. "I, um, had a boyfriend." She hesitated, dropping her gaze for a moment, and then smiled shyly. "But he never did that before."

Mystery solved—her ex was just a fucking selfish prick. What a damn shame, wasting a gorgeous woman's time in bed like that.

I smirked back at her. "He must have been a real dumbass then, especially if he let you slip away."

I thought I saw her expression darken for an instant, but before I could be sure of it, Lacey grinned mischievously and said, "I want to touch you too."

Well, a man certainly couldn't say no to that. I gladly lay back on the bed while she knelt down between my spread thighs. Watching her slim fingers tug down the zipper to my jeans was strangely erotic. I hadn't been undressed by a woman in a long time. Daniella's hands were generally bound, and so she rarely touched me. And though the last few years had been peppered by occasional one-night stands, I generally stripped as fast as I could to get to the main event.

A smile rose on my lips as I watched her carefully reach inside my boxers. I hadn't been treated with such delicacy in a long damn time, maybe ever. I wanted to joke that she didn't have to be so dainty with me, but I was transfixed; I could have watched her tentatively explore me for hours. And when her soft fist curled around me, I bit back a groan.

Using her other hand to push down my boxers, she freed my aching, swollen cock. Lacey sucked in a breath, her eyes darting up to mine. I knew I was hung, but her expression was priceless. She chewed on her lower lip, as if contemplating her task.

"You sure about this, sweetheart?" I asked at her hesitancy. I was going to have a hell of a case of blue balls if she changed her mind, but I'd live.

She swallowed, her pretty blue eyes drifting up to mine.

"Very." Then she gripped the base of my cock and, without hesitation, swallowed me down to her hand.

Fuuuck.

I groaned out loud. Pleasure shot through me, drawing my balls up close to my body as Lacey treated the head of my cock to a slow, wet kiss. Definitely *not* a virgin. Her tongue flicked in perfect rhythm with the bobbing of her head and the stroking of her hand on my shaft.

"You're good at this, baby." I stroked her silky brunette locks and she murmured, acknowledging the praise. "Mmm, just like that."

She kept up the perfect rhythm, not too fast, but not too slow either, her mouth creating a warm, wet suction over me.

I combed her hair away from her face with my fingers. I couldn't seem to stop petting her, touching her. Rubbed my hands along her shoulders and down her arms, tangled them in her hair, brushed my thumbs along her jaw, anything to let her know how amazing her mouth felt.

Letting my head fall back, I savored how the pleasure gradually burned higher and hotter in my groin. I watched Lacey's pink lips sliding over my wet cock. I wished she would look up at me, but she kept her sky-blue eyes closed, sooty lashes long on her flushed cheeks. Too shy to meet my gaze—though not too shy to suck the life out of me, apparently. *Hell, that feels good.*

My abs were already tensing with every stroke. In a minute, I panted, "I'm going to come soon."

But instead of pulling away at my warning, Lacey opened her eyes. *She wants to watch me come,* I realized—and arousal shocked through me like lightning. Arching slightly off the couch, I released with a low, ragged groan. Without a pause, she swallowed it.

This woman was becoming more perfect by the day. And that scared the fuck out of me.

Chapter Eleven

Lacey

After a long day at work, where confusing thoughts of Nolan had spun through my brain, all I wanted to do was to curl up on the couch and watch mindless TV while I ate dinner. But I had no groceries in the house, and since the last thing I felt like doing was grocery shopping and then cooking, I decided to call for takeout.

Vino's was a wine bar and bistro just a short drive away. My boss, Jamie, had suggested it when I asked if there were any good Italian restaurants in town. When I arrived, the parking lot was filled, which was surprising for a weeknight. *Their food must be even better than Jamie said.*

Inside, I learned why the place was really so crowded. A banner announced that the Nurses' Ball was to my left, in a private banquet room. I headed straight toward the bar, where I paid for my order and was told it would be ten more minutes.

I tried not to get annoyed. Ten more minutes until warm fettuccine Alfredo and garlicky breadsticks were in my tummy. I was hoping there was an empty seat at the bar—I could have a glass of wine while I waited, maybe text Brynn—but it was packed too. So I wandered over to the hostess station to wait for my name to be called.

But a very different voice called for me. A familiar masculine one.

"Lacey?"

I turned and spotted Nolan, looking devastatingly handsome in a black tuxedo and crisp white shirt. His black silk bowtie rested perfectly over the hollow of his throat. The unexpected sight stole my breath for a moment.

"Nolan? What are you doing here?"

He tipped his head toward the banquet room. "I'm here with Daniella."

I thought he might offer to introduce us, but he didn't. Which was fine by me. My heart was hammering against my ribs and all I wanted to do was flee. After the evening we'd spent together, the waltzing, the way he'd tugged down my wet panties and devoured me . . . I shuddered. And now he was here with *her*?

"I was just getting takeout," I explained, even though he hadn't asked.

He just stood there watching me, freshly shaved and smelling lightly of cologne. I couldn't take my eyes off him. The idea that he was here, on a date, with another woman was mind-boggling. As was the fact that he'd taken the time to dress up and look so handsome . . . for her, not me. It stung much more than I thought it would.

"I better get back in there before she comes looking for me," he said.

"Of course." I smiled, trying to shove down the tidal wave of jealousy inside me. "Have fun."

The words were a damn lie. I wanted him to have a terrible time, so terrible he ran straight into my arms without looking back. But I knew that wouldn't happen.

Nolan watched me sadly. "I'll call you later."

The bitter side of me wanted to tell him not to bother. But I stuffed those words down my throat and smiled instead. He'd been honest from the beginning. What did I expect?

I watched him walk into the elegant room with black-clothed tables and sconces dimmed low. He stopped beside a woman in a long green evening gown, and she whispered something in his ear. He nodded and patted her hand. And that was how I caught my first glimpse of Daniella.

Whenever I thought of the other woman in his life, it was always some abstract concept, a hazy figure. Something I could pretend was far away from me and my relationship with him. But the Daniella in front of me was all too solid and clear. She was a real person, with a profession and colleagues . . . and a pseudo-boyfriend she wanted to show off to them.

She took his elbow. Sensing they were coming closer, I faced the hostess station again and pressed my back to the wall, not wanting to be seen.

The image of them together was burned into my brain. She was nothing like how I pictured she'd be. She was tall— in her heels, almost as tall as Nolan. Her dark auburn hair was twisted into a sophisticated knot at the nape of her pale neck. I hadn't seen her face, which was a good thing. I didn't want to know if she was beautiful; my insecurity would crush me. Better to stay in the dark.

"See that guy over there with the dark hair and goatee?"

That low, faintly husky voice must be Daniella. They were only a few feet away now, just past the doorway I leaned against.

"What about him?" Nolan responded.

"He's a new doctor . . . and rumor has it, he's a Dominant."

"That guy?" Nolan asked in disbelief. "Dude doesn't have a Dominant bone in his body. Look at him."

Hearing their private conversation, how comfortable they were together, was startling. I was spying on a stolen moment between them. But I felt frozen in place, unable to move, barely even breathing.

"Don't be mean. Just because he's not built like a linebacker—or a SEAL, for that matter—doesn't mean anything. I've heard he's all varieties of naughty. He even joined the club downtown."

"You tempted?" Nolan sounded surprised.

"No, don't be crazy." Daniella laughed.

The sound was deep and husky. Sensual even. I *hated* the sound of it.

"I'm not suggesting anything crazy. Just that if you were interested, it could be a good thing. Get back on the horse, so to speak."

I could hear the hint of a smile in Nolan's voice, and I held my breath, wondering what she might say next.

"No, I have everything I need right here." She let out a contented little sigh that made my stomach hurt.

Nolan merely chuckled, sounding calm and jovial.

"Things have been weird lately, but . . . we're good, right?" she asked him.

"Of course we are," he said.

I couldn't stand to listen anymore. My insides felt like

they were being pulled out with a fork.

I pushed my way through the group lingering at the hostess station and out into the night air. Dinner forgotten, I got in my car and drove home to my empty little apartment.

• • •

When Nolan called that night, I was still feeling shaken and vulnerable. I picked up with a listless, "Hello?"

"Are you okay?"

Apparently, he understood that seeing him out with Daniella was a big deal to me. I sensed now that he'd been deliberately keeping us apart. We would probably never meet face-to-face. And that was fine by me.

I curled up into a warm nest on my bed, my purple quilt around my shoulders. "It was honestly . . . tough." Much tougher than I'd ever imagined.

He was quiet for a moment, just the sound of his deep, steady breaths on the other end of the phone. "I figured."

So he was calling to check on me, but not to end what had hurt me in the first place. He still wasn't ready to become a one-woman kind of man. Tears stung my eyes.

"Tell me what you're thinking," he said, his voice softer than I expected.

"There's this whole other side to your life that I'm not

involved in. Tuxedos and work banquets with coworkers. It was just . . . hard to take in."

"If it makes you feel any better, the tuxedo was uncomfortable as hell, and I couldn't wait to get out of it. I'm in my bedroom stripping down now."

"Are you alone?"

"No."

A single tear slipped down my cheek. "Oh."

"Sutton's here. He's giving me a dirty look."

And then I was laughing.

"I just need you to . . ." He didn't finish. But he didn't have to.

"I know."

Nolan needed me to accept him as he was—broken and all. And I did.

That's what scared me.

Chapter Twelve

Lacey

Scoop, then dump. Scoop, then dump.

I tried to hold my breath while cleaning the cat's litter box of clumps. It wasn't a glamorous job, but somebody had to do it. Thank God Mr. Wiggles had been declawed, because he was an angry son of a bitch.

Moving on to the small rodent cages, I threw away the old, dirty bedding and wiped down the floors with diluted bleach. Even the lowliest of rats deserved cozy nesting material, fresh water, and maybe a couple of extra pellets of food. I lost myself in my work, humming as I moved from cage to cage.

As hurt and confused as I'd been last night, seeing Nolan out with Daniella, an hour-long phone call had soothed me tremendously. He'd chatted with me while I lay in bed and he removed his tuxedo piece by piece. I heard the mattress creak as he lay down, heard Sutton softly snoring by his side.

Knowing that I was the one on his mind after his *date* didn't make everything better; bitter jealousy still lingered. But it had helped. We talked, laughed, and made plans to see each other again.

As I worked, I slipped back into daydreams of Nolan. The last few weeks had gone better than I'd ever imagined. With the exception of Daniella . . . but maybe, with some creativity, I could solve that problem too.

"You have all the signs of a woman in love," an old man's voice said.

"Excuse me?" I rose to my feet, securing the latch to the cage I'd just finished with, and turned to see Horace. He was one of the senior citizens who volunteered at the shelter on weekdays. I'd barely heard him come in.

"Your cheeks are rosy, your eyes are bright and happy, and you were humming a love song—Marvin Gaye, I think—while you scraped hamster shit from the bottom of that cage." He chuckled.

Panic hit me like a smack to the face. "No, it's nothing like that." *Of course not . . . right?*

My palms started to sweat. I was never supposed to give Nolan my heart. But somewhere between the moonlit walks, drinks, waltzing, and kissing, I had fallen for him. Completely. Overhearing him with Daniella last night only confirmed what I already knew. My heart wasn't just a little involved; it beat only for him.

Followed by that realization was the crushing guilt that

slammed into me over everything I'd been hiding from him.

Drawing a shaky breath, I met Horace's eyes.

"Been in love a time or two myself." He nodded. "I know the look."

"Excuse me," I muttered, brushing past him.

I pushed my way out the big metal door at the end of the hall, gulping down deep lungfuls of the fresh air outside. The smells were only slightly improved out here, since I was standing next to the dog run.

I thought about calling Brynn for advice. But what would she tell me that I didn't already know? That I was being an idiot? That a relationship built on deceit was doomed to fail?

Hearing those things out loud would make them more real, so I left my phone in my pocket. Brynn had always been pragmatic and straitlaced, every bit a daddy's girl. The last thing I needed to hear was the bitter disappointment in my sister's voice. I was disgusted enough with myself already. Thank you very much.

As I sank down into the dirt, I tried to remember that there was a method to my madness.

But once I'd actually met Nolan and stared up into his handsome blue eyes, it wasn't hard to feel something stir inside me. He was a protector, through and through. It didn't hurt how attractive he was with that strong, angular jawline, full lips, rugged muscles, and a filthy mouth too. I'd fallen hard and fast.

Even on that first night we talked, I knew this wasn't going to be cut and dried. I'd worn a polite smile and nodded along to his stories about leaving the Navy, moving back home to Texas to be near his mom, and working at a private security firm.

But when the conversation had turned to his fallen friend, the look in his eyes had darkened, and a knot of unease had settled in my stomach. What had started as a game or a silly dare had become very real.

In my mind, Nolan Maxwell had been a one-dimensional ex-Navy SEAL badass who could offer me the protection I needed. The reality was that he was a real human being with battle wounds, hidden depths, and a soft side for women. He had invited me into his life—a life he already shared with another. And now I wanted more.

He'd been nothing but forthcoming, all while I dodged questions about my past and hid the truth from him.

So here I was, sitting in the dirt, fearful of what was to come. Once he knew my secret, that would be the end of it.

He'd go back to his quiet, happy life with Daniella. But didn't he deserve more? And didn't I?

Thinking about the times we'd spent together, gazing into his handsome face, his eyes as deep and blue as the ocean . . . *God*, it was all burned into my brain. Every erotic moment replayed like an old movie I'd memorized from watching too many times.

It seemed that massaging Nolan's tight, weary muscles had made all my feelings rush to the surface. He'd seemed in awe of me, as if he'd never had a woman care for him that way. And the tender way we'd touched and caressed each other's flesh until we came together . . . it was indescribable. The most sensual thing I'd ever done by far. I had no regrets about that.

I wanted to care for this man, including all his broken bits. Nurse his wounded heart back to life. It had lain dormant for so long.

Maybe it was just wishful thinking, but I had the inkling that Daniella's presence in his life was a Band-Aid, a sorry excuse for the real thing. She didn't love him. Not if she was okay sharing him. If Daniella truly cared for him the way he deserved, she'd never be okay with my presence in his life, another woman's perfume on his skin or name on his lips.

I sure as hell wasn't—and I'd known him mere weeks,

not years like her.

"Lacey?" Horace poked his head out the door to peer down on me. "You okay?"

I wiped my eyes with the back of my hand. *Stupid tears.*

"Just a sec," I called. It wasn't fair to hide out here.

Horace nodded once. A moment later, the big door thudded shut.

I pushed my hands into my hair and hung my head between my knees. *Fuck. What was I thinking?*

I knew exactly what I'd been thinking. That I was in trouble back home, and Nolan was the man who could keep me safe.

If I'd known then just how dangerous this whole thing would become, I might have gotten into my car and driven straight back to Oklahoma. Instead, I picked myself up from the ground, dusted off my jeans, and headed back inside to finish my shift with the nosy but well meaning Horace.

Chapter Thirteen

Nolan

Things were beginning to feel more strained than ever between Daniella and me, and I was no closer to figuring out what was going on with Lacey and me. Getting shit-faced with Grey hadn't helped, either. I just wasn't ready to think about changing my future. Every scenario twisted my stomach with unease.

And then I'd spent that incredible evening with Lacey. Watching her attempt to waltz, feeling her warm mouth on me . . .

If I turned my life upside-down for her, what then? End up just like the others I'd watched crash and burn as they sought their happily-ever-after? *Fuck that.*

Still, the harder I tried to hold on to the way things had always been, the more uneasy I felt. I couldn't deny any longer that Daniella and I were drifting apart. While I'd fulfilled my obligation by taking her to the Nurses' Ball, we hadn't hung out in a long time, and I hadn't played with her in even longer.

Our once-tranquil relationship was starting to fray at the edges. She needed release, and even though she was trying to give me space, she probably felt snubbed. Ignored—and ultimately replaced with a younger woman. Just like her last Dom had done.

Even if her body didn't excite me anymore, I still had a sense of loyalty toward her. And Daniella had always given me what I needed; I couldn't desert her just because someone new had come into my life. It wasn't like I was ready to commit to Lacey and be monogamous. *Was I?* But if this tension kept up, I might lose my mind.

"Have you seen my Navy sweatshirt?" I asked Daniella as she passed by my door. I'd just spent fifteen minutes tearing my room apart looking for the damn thing.

"Yeah, in my closet, I think," she said, heading toward the living room with a book in hand.

I should have known. The sweatshirt was a good ten years old, soft and thin from so many washings. It was my—and Daniella's—favorite thing to wear in the fall.

Stalking into her room, I found it on the floor of her closet underneath a heap of dirty clothes. *Wow, real fucking nice, Dani.*

"It smells like girly shit," I complained loud enough for her to hear. I took the shirt back to my room, threw it in the hamper, and grabbed another from my closet.

"Geez, what crawled up your ass?"

"Nothing, all right? Everything's fine." It was a lie. Nothing was fine right now.

"I'm going to make beef stew for dinner."

"Okay." My tone softened. Her homemade stew was my favorite thing that Daniella made. She was trying to smooth over this growing weirdness between us. That was more than I could say for myself.

"Dinner will be in about an hour," she added.

"Sounds good."

I headed back to my room, deciding a hot shower might calm my frayed nerves. I stripped and turned on the water, feeling impatient and restless. I'd always been a fixer. It was how I ended up with Daniella—and Sutton, for that matter— but it sounded more chivalrous then it was.

I was no one's hero. I'd always known that the second you let your guard down and did something stupid like fall in love, you got fucked, your world ripped out from underneath you. Like what happened to Marcus. Daniella. My mom.

Shit, maybe lack of sex was clouding my brain. I wasn't fucking Dani, and I sure as shit wasn't fucking Lacey.

Lacey. The new woman who'd waltzed in and taken my life by storm. Or, if you listened to the way Grey told it, the woman who had me by the balls.

As I waited for the water to heat, it occurred to me that I knew next to nothing about Lacey. Her background, her family, why she moved out of state just to work part-time at an animal shelter. But I knew exactly what she tasted like. How she felt moving on top of me. The noises she made when she came.

Fuck.

Something was starting to pick at me about this whole situation, but I couldn't pinpoint what, and my mind raced with unanswered questions.

• • •

After dinner, I was still no closer to an answer. As I sat at the kitchen table with my laptop and a whiskey, Sutton snoring lightly at my feet, I heard a low moan come from Daniella's bedroom.

At least one of us is having fun.

Half working, half surfing the web, I ignored her groans, trying to give her some privacy. Until I realized that if she'd left her bedroom door open, it was probably on purpose.

Standing up from the table, I stretched and stepped around Sutton, headed down the hall that led to her room.

Daniella was naked, kneeling in the center of her

bedroom floor. Her hands were linked behind her back. She was presenting herself to me, offering her submission as a gift.

I wondered how long she'd been waiting for me to find her. We'd finished dinner over an hour ago.

Shit.

I stepped forward, about to yank her up from her spot on the floor, tell her we couldn't do this. Not when so much hung in the balance. Until I realized . . . I couldn't. I didn't have the heart.

Her eyes found mine, and I could read everything in them as plain as day. In those soft hazel depths, I saw it clearly. If I denied her right now, it would crush her. And not just the sting of rejection that would fade in a day or two. Refusing her offering might mean her sinking back into the depression I'd barely pulled her out of two years ago.

Fuck.

I couldn't do that to her. For now, at least, she was still my responsibility.

"Eyes on the floor," I ordered.

Her shoulders relaxed, her spine dipping as if my words had caressed her.

Bending down, I secured a blindfold over her eyes. I

didn't want to feel their penetrating gaze on me as I worked. Then I helped her stand and guided her to the bed.

Once I bent her over my knee, I could feel the heat of her skin through my jeans. I noticed her fist was clenched around something.

"Open your hand," I ordered.

She did. A small stainless steel butt plug rested in her palm. She wasn't leaving much guessing room about what she wanted, or needed, tonight.

"Look at you," I growled. "Offering yourself to me. On display like this."

I took the plug from her and slowly stroked the cold steel down her spine, over the cleft of her ass, raising a trail of goose bumps.

Daniella shuddered.

Her biggest kink was bondage—exposure, helplessness, objectification—and I knew how to hit it hard. The sight of her presenting herself to me didn't stir my cock like it used to, but I could still give her what she needed.

I slowly pushed the plug into her ass, pausing whenever her breath caught, then easing forward again when she adjusted to the stretch. When I'd worked it in all the way to its flared base, I patted her hip in silent praise.

I brought my hand down against her bare ass—soft taps at first and then harder, until my palm cracked against her skin. The forceful blows jostled the plug in her ass, sending sparks through her every nerve.

Daniella cried out with each slap, a wild, shapeless noise of pure sensation, before whimpering out loud. Her voice grew fuzzier and her body relaxed as she sank further into subspace.

I was concentrating so hard that I didn't hear the knock at the front door. I didn't hear the soft footsteps down the hall, the creak of the bedroom door swinging open.

But I did hear the startled gasp.

I whipped my head around to see Lacey frozen in the bedroom doorway. Her hand was clamped over her mouth. Her wide eyes darted back and forth over the lurid scene— me, a naked Daniella draped across my lap, spanking the shit out of her red ass.

Lacey's expression hit me like a gut punch; I could barely breathe. In her eyes, I saw pure horror and heartbreak. She was so scared, so disgusted—and it was all because of me. In that moment, I hated what I saw in her eyes.

Then she ran, darting out of the room just as quickly as she'd appeared.

I eased Daniella off my lap and onto the bed, and she

gave a soft sigh. When I pulled off her blindfold, she looked drained, drowsy, as she rested her head on the pillow.

Daniella was riding a serious endorphin high, swaddled in the warm fog of subspace. As badly as I wanted to go after Lacey, I knew I had to handle Daniella's aftercare first.

I brought her a mug of hot, sugary tea, sat with her while she drank it, and rubbed her back until she fell asleep.

Then I wrote her a note—*Let's talk in the morning*—and left it on her nightstand. It was kind of a cold move, but I had to do some damage control before Lacey freaked out even worse. Or called the police on me.

I had no idea what she could be thinking. What she'd just witnessed had obviously confused and frightened her. I thought I'd made Daniella's kinky desires clear before . . . but evidently, being aware of BDSM was different from stumbling into a scene up close.

Did Lacey think I was a monster now? How much of our relationship could I salvage?

Hardly daring to hope, I hurried outside toward my truck, hell bent on getting to her apartment.

Chapter Fourteen

Lacey

Uncontrollable shaking racked my body. Anger. Fear. Disappointment. Confusion. *Jealousy*. The sheer number of emotions warring for my attention were overwhelming.

I paced my living room, my hands still trembling. It was a miracle I'd driven home without crashing. Tonight, on my way home from work, I'd spotted that same white sedan in my rearview mirror, and I panicked.

Instead of leading him to my home, I'd driven straight to Nolan's. I heard the TV playing inside and let myself in when there was no answer at the door. The last thing I expected was to interrupt a scene between him and Daniella.

The scent of sex was burned into my nostrils. As was the sight of Daniella, bound and blindfolded, her ass splotchy with large red handprints. *Nolan's handprints.*

Chills swept down my spine as I leaned against the dining room table for support, unable to banish the vision from my brain. My fingers curled around the edge of the table and I drew a few deep breaths, trying to calm my rioting heartbeat.

My own visceral reaction to seeing them startled me with

its intensity. I'd told myself all along that I didn't care what they did in bed, but now I knew that had been a bald-faced lie.

The reason it mattered so much? The reason my heart felt like it had just been ripped in two?

Horace had been right—I was falling in love with Nolan. And seeing him with Daniella not only hurt like a bitch, but it made me panic about losing him. They obviously shared something that he and I never would.

One thing that was odd . . . I suddenly realized Nolan had been fully clothed.

Before I had time to dissect that, a series of knocks rained against my door. Startled and still shaking, I hazarded a glance out the peephole.

It was Nolan. Veins stood out against his neck, and his blue eyes were so dark, they looked almost black.

"I know you're in there," he said. "Let me in. We need to talk."

Shit. I wasn't sure I could face him right now, but I had no choice.

I unbolted the lock and opened the door.

"Are you okay?"

The first words out of his mouth caught me off guard. I'd expected some backlash over me just wandering inside his house, or a lecture about how I knew the score all along and had no right to be mad. Instead he seemed genuinely concerned. For *me*.

I shoved a hand against his chest, pushing him back a step. "No, I'm not okay."

Unable to meet his dark eyes, I turned away and stalked over to the window, where I looked down at the parking lot. Watching the old lady from unit 6D take out her trash was better than letting Nolan see me cry.

"Fuck," he muttered.

He crossed the room to sink down on the couch. He looked so out of place on the dainty, floral-patterned thing, I would have laughed if my stomach weren't tied in knots. His large frame, muscular build, and strong jaw dusted with a five o'clock shadow was at odds with my feminine apartment, with its splashes of purple and cream everywhere.

I turned to face him, my hands on my hips. "It's stupid, right? I knew from the beginning that you'd never be mine. But silly me, somewhere along the way, I started to think maybe, just maybe you'd want more . . . with me. But now I see that—"

"You see what?"

My eyes flared on his. "That if *those* are the kinds of things you're into, I'll never be able to give you what you need."

"Damn it, Lacey. I'd never make you feel like you had to do those things."

Something between a gasp and a forced laugh escaped my throat. "You're an asshole, Nolan."

"I need to explain some things to you. Will you sit down?"

I was so angry that my skin felt hot all over, but something inside me needed to hear whatever asinine excuse he was about to come up with.

"Fine." I sank onto the couch beside him.

He scrubbed a hand over the back of his neck. "Daniella's a submissive."

"You already told me that." My voice was flat and emotionless. If he was going to rehash this shit, I was going to kick him out on his ass.

"Yes, but what that means is that she needs discipline, punishment, restraint. That's what you saw tonight. It wasn't sex. In fact, I haven't slept with her since you came here."

My gaze snapped over to his. *Okay, that was unexpected.*

"Why?"

"Good fucking question."

"What I saw was pretty damn sexual if you ask me," I spat back.

The woman had been completely nude, with an *instrument* of some type in her anus. I was assuming Nolan had been the one to put it there.

"Fair enough." He swallowed. "But seriously, I need you to know that I'd never ask you to do what you saw tonight."

Quiet and contemplative for a moment, I dared a glance up into his eyes. "I never said I wasn't willing. Maybe if I understood it, and I ... had the right partner ..." I swallowed, unsure what I was even asking for.

Based on his expression, I'd just shocked the shit out of him.

He took a moment to compose himself, seemingly unsure of how to proceed. Then he took my hand, stroking his thumb along the back of my knuckles.

"Still, I don't *need* kinky sex. I wouldn't want you to feel like you had to do something that made you uncomfortable or confused. I liked the tender moments we've shared. I've liked going slow with you, which, trust me, is totally out of character for me."

Still confused, my heart still aching, I watched him with guarded eyes, waiting for him to continue, waiting for any of this to make sense.

"What you saw tonight was what Daniella needs, so I provide it. When she came to me, broken and alone, I just . . ."

"It's okay, you don't have to explain."

I knew Nolan's protective side was fiercely loyal. He'd been filling a role Daniella needed. Nothing more. But he'd also completely closed himself off to love, and that was my real issue with Daniella's presence in his life.

"I'll explain anything you want me to. I've tried to be up front about all this from the beginning."

"Do you love her?" The words startled me, leaping from my mouth without permission. I held my breath, waiting for him to answer.

With a deep line etched between his brows, he met my worried stare. "I don't know. She's my friend and I care for her. We've been there for each other for a long time."

I nodded. Two years was a long time. Attachments had been made.

"You're my light, my warmth, and my sunshine," he continued, stroking my hand. "You chase away the shadows in me. And she's my dark, submitting to every wicked desire I have inside me. My yin and my yang."

I didn't want to be someone's yin or yang. I wanted to be his everything. And suddenly I felt angry. I wanted to snatch my hand away and make him leave . . .

Until the guilt of my own secret weighed down on me, reminding me that I had no right to judge him and his lifestyle when my being here had all been based on a lie.

But even though it had started that way, real feelings had developed. My heart was on the line now.

"Are you asking me to choose?" he asked.

Blood pumped faster in my veins. *What if he chooses her?*

"I just . . . just need time to think," I stammered. I would rather take my chances with the bad guys than give an ultimatum to a man who didn't want me.

"I know this situation is a little fucked. Trust me, I get that. If there's anything I can do, anything else you need, please tell me."

I nodded. Despite Nolan's flaws—like having one too many women in his life—I respected him. He was protective, dependable, and trustworthy. And a whole slew of other qualities I really needed in my life right now. My stupid heart told me to just hang on. That maybe, *just maybe*, he would be mine when he got over his fear of commitment and losing someone he cared for.

"There's something else you need to know," he said, his tone soft and low.

Oh Christ. What now?

"What's that?"

Stroking my cheek with his calloused thumb, he leaned closer. "I've never kissed Daniella."

My breathing stopped for a moment. "Ever?"

"Never," he confirmed.

Knowing that intimacy was something he'd shared only with me caused a little spark of hope to flare in my chest.

Then Nolan pulled me close, bringing my mouth to his. He kissed me slowly, softly, without any rush. It was tender, and sweet, and loving. And it made my head spin with confusion.

This entire situation was the definition of a *clusterfuck*.

Chapter Fifteen

Nolan

Early the next morning, I was cooking breakfast when Daniella wandered out in her pajamas, rubbing her eyes. Usually she came out of her room fully dressed, if she had to be somewhere soon, or wearing her lounging-around sweatpants. She must be feeling crappy today.

Damn it, that was almost certainly my fault. But what else could I have done? Last night would have been a disaster no matter what.

"You get my note?" I asked.

Sutton snuffled the floor around me, smearing his cold, wet nose on my bare feet. I accidentally-on-purpose dropped a chunk of hash browns for him. He gulped it down in a blink.

Daniella sat down at the dining table, eyeing the full pan in my hand. "Yep."

Damn, this was awkward. Knowing I needed to forge ahead, I served up two heaping plates and two mugs of coffee, then sat across from her. Sutton lay down on my foot, poised to snatch up any more scraps.

"Listen," I began, not really knowing how to end. "Last

night was . . ."

Daniella stared down into her mug, stirring cream into her coffee. "You weren't into it."

Automatically, I shook my head, but my denial caught in my throat. I'd never once lied to her, and I wasn't about to start now.

"It wasn't just that. Things have been . . . weird lately. And then last night, finding you in your room like that . . ." I had to drag every word out of my throat.

Fuck.

Her hazel eyes met mine as she waited for me to continue, waited to understand what could possibly be going on with me that I didn't want to fuck a primed, ready, and willing woman.

I cleared my throat. "Lacey ended up stopping by, and she saw us from the doorway."

"Oh. I didn't know that."

I nodded. "I'm sorry."

The apology felt insincere, but then again, I hadn't planned on last night's scene with Daniella. The door being unlocked wasn't really anyone's fault. Or maybe I wasn't ready to face the fact that the two women in my life were colliding in a way I'd never planned on.

So I left it at that. I couldn't understand my own feelings, let alone explain this crisis to anyone else. I just stuffed a forkful of scrambled eggs into my mouth. I could hear Sutton wheezing slightly in the silence.

Daniella poured a ribbon of ketchup over her hash browns, watching the red dribble with exaggerated care, keeping her gaze downcast. "Yeah, last night I could tell . . . you weren't just not into the scene. You weren't into me."

Ouch. I almost winced. Not "you weren't into the scene," but "you weren't into me." And no soothing noises like "but it's okay, I understand" to soften the blow.

We'd always been pretty blunt with each other, so I knew she wasn't trying to guilt-trip me, just stating the facts. I usually found her straightforwardness refreshing. And it would be shitty to expect Daniella to reassure me about hurting her feelings, anyway.

But her words couldn't help but sting. It was hard not to notice the chill in the air, the too-long pauses, the stiff, rehearsed way she sipped her coffee. As if our whole conversation was a bad movie.

"Yeah," I finally admitted. "I wasn't. Things have been kind of fucked lately." Understatement. Things were totally FUBAR.

She nodded. "I noticed."

Did I hear a note of sadness in her voice? Or was it anger?

Desperate to get the hell away from this topic, I added, "Anyway, I went and talked to Lacey after she left. She's not upset anymore." Fuck, that sounded bad. I wet my lips. "I mean, I don't think she was ever really upset. Just . . . startled."

Daniella smiled with obvious relief. It was small and a little wan, but it was the most genuine expression I'd seen on her face in a while. "Good to know we didn't traumatize her."

Reaching down to rub Sutton's back, I considered going into more detail about last night. But the thought of sharing such an intimate conversation . . . I really didn't want to. It felt wrong, damaging, like the things I'd revealed to Lacey would wither in the light of day. But my private talk with her still felt like another secret I was keeping from Daniella. Yet another brick in the growing wall between us.

In uncomfortable silence, we finished the last of our breakfast, facing each other across an invisible divide.

After breakfast, Daniella cleaned the dishes while I grabbed my laptop and headed into the office, needing to escape the weird vibe in our house.

· · ·

Later that afternoon, Lacey invited me over for a drink. *I want to talk to you,* her short text had said.

A message like that was never good news. With every step from my truck to her apartment, my foreboding deepened. But when Lacey opened her door, still dressed in workout clothes from her run, I started to relax. She was so down to earth and easy to be around, it calmed me.

After a brief hello, she gestured to the couch. I sat down and she went to the kitchen to pour our drinks. She came back with a glass of lemon iced tea for herself and a tumbler of whiskey for me.

I took a sip; it was perfect, with just enough water to bring out the whiskey's full flavor. She hadn't struck me as a hard-liquor fan, so she must have bought a bottle just for me. And she remembered exactly how I liked it.

"How are you?" Lacey asked, her blue eyes bright and fixed on me.

Trying to keep my balance in an earthquake. "I'm fine. Are you still okay?"

She nodded. "Yeah. I'm sorry I got so mad last night. I guess I just ... I felt too much, and it surprised me. Everything all came out in the worst way."

I reached out, wanting to take her hand and soothe her guilt. But she wasn't finished.

Looking down at her cup, she bit her lip. "Seeing you like that made me realize something."

Shit. I knew what she was about to say. The heavy atmosphere felt dark and inescapable.

"At first, I thought I could do this . . ." Lacey waved her hand, distressed, searching for the right words. "Sharing you with someone else. But it turns out I can't."

I exhaled slowly, trying to keep control. Fear and anger whirled through me all at once, squeezing my heart and roiling my stomach.

"Nolan?" She rested her hand on my arm. Her gentle touch, meant to reassure, burned my skin and clouded my thoughts. "I'm sorry to put you in this position. I didn't want to force you to choose, like some kind of ultimatum."

I forced myself to say something more coherent than swearing. "No, it's okay. I know you're not doing this to manipulate me. If you want monogamy, then that's what you want."

I wasn't lying—I didn't blame Lacey at all. Coming clean was much better than hiding her needs behind a plastic smile, getting more and more resentful, until our whole relationship blew up in my face. But knowing that didn't help my feelings right now. Mainly because I had no fucking idea what I was going to do.

She nodded and a tentative smile appeared. "I'm glad you understand. I feel bad, but it's just, realistically, I know I can't go on like this."

I knew what she was talking about. My bond and obligations to Daniella pulled me away. To give Lacey my full attention—which was what she needed from a lover—I would have to cut those ties and make Lacey a higher priority.

On some level, way in the back of my mind, I'd known this moment was coming. But feeling the gathering tension in the air hadn't prepared me for the storm. I was caught between a rock and a hard place—a submissive who trusted and relied on me, and a new lover who I wanted more with.

And while I definitely felt something for Lacey, something real and good and pure, I'd have to sell my soul to hold on to it. And there was no fucking way I was ready to do that. Not now, possibly not ever.

Choosing Lacey meant uprooting my whole carefully constructed life. My independence, my simple pleasures, my freedom from pain. But not choosing her . . . the thought felt like a knife between the ribs.

Uncomfortable, I shifted, searching for a way to make

her understand. "I told you in the beginning how I operated, what I was looking for."

"You have feeling in that closed-off heart of yours," she said, her voice cracking with emotion. "I've seen it. When you talk about those kids at the camp . . ."

"No. That's just my way of ensuring one less kid falls down the rocky path I did. It's nothing; trust me."

Her eyes said something different.

Trapped, confused, I told her I needed to think and got the hell out of there.

As I drove toward town, I texted Greyson. *Meet me at West's?* Even if he didn't offer any useful advice, I could still get black-out drunk.

● ● ●

As soon as I sat down next to him at the bar, Greyson said, "Let me guess. This is about Lacey again."

"Hello to you too, asshole."

The bartender came over, and I ordered a whiskey.

Greyson took a slug of his beer. "What's the situation?"

I gave him a quick recap of everything that had happened in the past twenty-four hours, including Lacey's final decision about monogamy.

"So, congratulations, you were right," I finished sourly.

"Damn." Greyson sighed. "That's some heavy shit."

I glared at him in exasperation. "I'm so glad for your infinite wisdom."

Greyson shrugged, turning his palms up. "What do you want me to say? You're in a tough place, and I can see why you're stressing out, but the solution is kind of obvious. Right?"

Obvious? The hell is he talking about?

When I didn't respond for a minute, his eyes widened into an incredulous stare. "Dude. Are you serious? You have this incredible connection with Lacey, and you're still going to keep fucking around?"

"I didn't say that," I snapped. "I came to talk to you because I don't know what I'm going to do. This isn't as simple as you seem to think."

"I think you could love Lacey. I know you don't love Daniella." Greyson shrugged again and almost spilled a little of his beer. "Sounds pretty damn simple to me."

I didn't even want to address his use of the L-word. The motherfucker.

"Just because we're not romantic doesn't mean Daniella isn't important to me. We've been friends for years. I can't just ditch her."

My whiskey chose that moment to arrive. I threw a ten at the bartender and said, "Keep the change," impatient to finish before Grey could interrupt. "If you got a girlfriend and suddenly stopped hanging out with me, that would make you a tool."

"But I'm not fucking you, am I?" Greyson laughed at his own joke. "And you're not just 'hanging out' with Daniella. Sex kinda changes the equation." He pinched his thumb and finger together. "Just a little."

Why did Greyson have to be so goddamn annoying when he was right? "Yeah, but Daniella needs me. I give her a place to live. I'd be throwing her out on the street."

"Oh, please. She's only living with you for free because you insisted. She'll be fine on her own. Nurses make pretty decent money, and she's had two years to squirrel away almost all her paychecks. And it's not like Lacey would insist that you evict her without warning."

I bit my tongue. Greyson had no idea what he was talking about. My arrangement with Daniella wasn't just about money. She needed security and stability and emotional support. She also needed kink, and because of her asshole ex-Dom, I was the only person she trusted enough to submit to.

The ugly aftermath of her breakup two years ago was still in play now.

But none of that was any of Greyson's business. I couldn't blab Daniella's whole private, painful history just to make a point. And deserting her in a time of need would make me an ass.

Greyson interrupted my stony silence. "Actually, screw this. Daniella's a big girl. Why not talk to her directly, instead of just talking about her?"

Because that would make this mess feel way too real. Because it meant my whole life was poised on the edge of a cliff. I struggled to come up with an explanation that wouldn't make Grey laugh in my face.

Eyes narrowed, I folded my arms over my chest. "I'm not doing that." Bringing this up now would only make her worry. I would tell her when I had a final decision.

"Damn it, Nolan," Grey muttered. For a long moment, he just stared at me, a somber expression on his face and his beer paused halfway to his mouth. I couldn't tell what he was thinking. "Holding a friend as he died in your arms would fuck anyone up."

Oh, hell no. He of all people did *not* get to throw that in my face.

"This has nothing to do with Marcus," I growled.

"The fuck it doesn't." Finally, Grey set down his glass and spun on the bar stool to face me fully. "You want my honest opinion or not?"

I shrugged. *Sure, why the hell not?*

"I think you're an idiot. You've got a woman who loves you, and you're sitting here wringing your hands about it to me. If you end things with Daniella, you can still hang out with her. She'll still be your friend with her clothes on. But if you end things with Lacey, you lose all of her. Everything your relationship could have been. A whole future full of possibilities. And you'll regret blowing that chance for the rest of your life."

"You don't know that," I muttered.

"Tell me one thing you like about Lacey, and would genuinely miss if she wasn't in your life."

I thought it over for a good long while. There was more than one thing . . . a lot more. Which might have been his entire point in asking me.

"She likes kissing me. A lot," I finally answered, feeling like a sentimental prick as a smug grin tugged up my lips.

"And Daniella doesn't?" He chuckled.

He really had no idea about the kink. Our relationship wasn't built on that kind of emotional intimacy. Just a fuckload of trust. She provided what I needed, and I gave her the same in return.

"No," I said simply.

Grey looked at me with a sort of sad gleam in his eye. Like he was happy I found someone who loved me enough to kiss me. *Openly. On the mouth. All the time.*

But shit, it wasn't like he had anyone, either. I knew he didn't have anyone warming his bed and loving on him. He spent all his time at work or at the gym. When he occasionally took a girl home, I never heard of her again.

"I think you have your answer, dude." He looked at me knowingly.

I grunted in acknowledgment, just to end this fucking conversation already. Little did he know I wasn't about to trade in my whole world for some good pussy.

We finished our drinks in silence for the next half hour. There was no escape from my own thoughts.

Grey didn't understand that I would lose more than sex if I ended things with Daniella. She represented my entire way of life for the past two years. My partner, my counterweight. We shared the same purpose. We could fulfill each other's needs for sex and companionship without getting attached enough to get hurt.

Until I met Lacey, I could have maintained that equilibrium forever. But she'd knocked me off-balance. And if I let those scales tip, there was no going back, whatever my new life had in store.

But, I realized, it was already too late. I'd reached the point of no return. Discontent had already crept into me. I'd tasted what a woman's love could offer, and the life that had once satisfied me now left me cold and hungry. Lacey promised me more, and even if I wasn't sure, did I really want to remain in this lukewarm limbo?

Last night, when Lacey had caught me in bed with Daniella and run away, my panic had left no room for confusion. Seeing Lacey like that had driven out every other thought. The idea that she might be scared or hurt had made me run after her on pure instinct. In that moment, my priorities had turned crystal clear.

And if the situations were reversed, I would never be okay with sharing Lacey with another man. The thought alone made me feel homicidal. Knowing someone else was touching her? It made me want to beat the motherfucker within an inch of his life.

But I wasn't about to tell Grey that he was right . . . and face every emotion I'd turned off. At least, not yet.

Chapter Sixteen

Lacey

I hadn't heard from Nolan in two days. Worry and doubt hadn't just *started* to creep in; they took over every cell of my being, settling in and demanding attention. I felt achy and tired all the time, despite sleeping more than usual.

Knowing I'd put him in a difficult spot with Daniella, I felt terrible asking him to decide. He'd been up front from the beginning, I'd known about her the entire time, and Daniella hadn't done anything wrong. Yet now I was asking him to essentially kick her out and give me exclusivity when I hadn't even been honest about my own past yet.

That would come. I knew it had to, but for now, I couldn't deny myself what I wanted. What was that saying? *The heart wants what it wants.* And mine wanted Nolan.

A simple phone call to him could solve all of my worry. I could ask him point-blank where he stood, what he wanted, and if he'd made a decision. But doubt and fear kept me from making that call. *What if he chooses her?*

I decided to take a chance. To finally meet Daniella, talk woman to woman, and see if we could settle this. Mustering up my courage, I headed downstairs and drove to Nolan's house.

When I pulled up, I was relieved to see his truck gone, and Daniella's little silver sedan parked in the driveway.

Here goes nothing.

Daniella opened the door with a warm smile. "Can I help you?"

Seeing her in person was like a smack of harsh realization to the face. She was beautiful. Tall with willowy limbs, and dark hair that hung down her back in loose waves. Her eyes couldn't be described as hazel, but they weren't quite brown either. Their mossy color was unique, and set against her porcelain skin and regal features, they were striking.

She was watching me with a guarded smile. Hidden in the smile was a question: *Are you going to change my entire world?*

But I didn't know the answer to that question. I took a deep breath and steeled myself for what was sure to be an awkward encounter.

"I'm Lacey."

Her smile instantly faded. "Nolan's not here right now."

My heart started to race. "I know that," I managed to say.

"Then, what brings you by?" Her tone held the same caution as her smile.

"I came by to see if I could talk to you, actually," I said, trying not to sound too panicked or aggressive.

"Okay," she replied—a little carefully.

She opened the door wider and I stepped into their neat living room. Vacuum lines in the carpet. Stacks of paperbacks that must have been hers sat on the bookshelves, resting beside his collection of vinyl records and various military awards.

A pit of unease settled in my stomach. For better or worse, they had built a life together.

"You want something to drink? A bottle of water?" she asked.

I nodded as she led the way through the kitchen, where she grabbed two bottles of water and then stopped at the dining table.

I sat down across from her and folded my hands in my lap. You could have cut the tension in the air with a knife. Especially since the images of her from that night were still burned into my brain, lurid and shocking.

Crimson streaks laced through her otherwise jet-black hair. Red handprints on her ass, tattoos twining over her skin, silver barbells in her nipples.

This woman and I were polar opposites. I was about as exotic as a slice of white bread. Nolan might have said that his relationship with Daniella was built solely on companionship, but obviously *something* about her turned him on. Even after just a few minutes in her presence, I could see why. She was different, exciting and edgy. Her lips were glossy red, she was wearing a faded T-shirt for a London Art Fair, and there was a tiny semicolon tattoo on the inside of her wrist.

I knew right then that this wasn't some meaningless affair. This woman had held his interest and dominated his love life for two years. Nobody else had even come close to her level of commitment.

Except for me . . . *God, I hope so.*

Sitting at Daniella's table—at *their* table—made me nervous in a way I hadn't been before. It was the shock I'd felt at the Nurses' Ball all over again. Every time I saw her, she became more of a real person to me; it was clear that she was no one-dimensional fling. She had interests and passions and depth. Their relationship had its own history that I couldn't touch. They had probably shared things that he and I never would—both in the bedroom and outside it.

A chill of icy dread crept over me. This wasn't going to be as easy as I'd hoped. I'd been so sure that Nolan and I were great together, but now, for the first time, I began to wonder if *I* measured up. If I was enough for him.

Daniella watched me coolly but with equal interest, no doubt wondering what Nolan saw in me.

My heart rate accelerated. *Shit. Maybe coming here was a mistake after all.* Taking a deep breath, I stuck to the plan.

"First, I have to apologize for barging in the other day. I heard voices and let myself inside, never dreaming that I'd interrupt . . . something between you and Nolan."

I didn't mention that I was being followed. I didn't mention that I'd feared for my safety. I just let them think I was a presumptuous person who went barging into people's houses. It felt awfully brash and brazen now, but at the time, it had seemed like my only option.

Her eyes settled on mine, but she waved a dismissive hand. "I had no idea, honestly . . . my mind was elsewhere. But Nolan told me after, and he said he went to check on you. Are you okay?"

"Actually, no." My gaze darted up to Daniella's. "But not because of what I saw. Your kink is your business. It's just that seeing Nolan with another woman made me realize . . . how deeply my feelings for him ran."

"I see." Daniella shifted uncomfortably in her seat. "What are you saying?"

The room spun with unspoken tension and emotion. I wiped my damp palms on my jeans.

"I gave him a choice. Told him what I want—me and him, an exclusive relationship."

Daniella laughed abruptly, a humorless burst of shocked surprise, as if she couldn't believe what she was hearing. "What did he say?"

"He's still thinking it over. I'm not sure what he wants." My voice grew quiet, my own doubts obvious in my tone. "I'm not sure if my ultimatum will drive a wedge between us, or if it will mean the end for you and him."

Daniella's eyes widened just slightly, but enough for me to know that the idea scared her. "So you couldn't handle it after all . . . us fucking the same man."

I twisted my hands in my lap. "Actually, Nolan and I . . . we haven't had sex."

Daniella's posture stiffened as the color drained from her face. "Well, that changes everything."

"How so?"

"Because that's not how Nolan operates. Never has. I thought you were a random booty call, someone to give him the vanilla he liked on the side. But if you haven't even slept with him, it's obvious he has real feelings for you."

Simultaneous hope and dread bloomed inside my chest. The beginning of a real relationship with Nolan meant everything to me, but it would also mean coming clean about my past. Whether I was ready or not.

"Listen," Daniella said, "if this is what you want, and if it's what *he* wants, I'm not going to stand in the way. Ultimately, it's up to Nolan."

I nodded.

Now, we would just have to wait and see.

Chapter Seventeen

Stuffing the essentials into a black duffel bag, I go over my plan again. Rope. *Check*. Zip ties. *Check*. Directions to get the fuck out of town if this goes south. *Check*.

The desire for revenge boils under my skin. I'm hot, edgy, and unsatisfied. Vengeance is now so close I can taste it in the air.

If circumstances had been different, if you'd followed what you were supposed to do . . . maybe I could have made this easier on you. But there's no going back now. I'll see to it that you suffer.

You ruined what I once held dear. Ruined everything I built for myself. And now you're going to pay. I'm almost giddy with excitement, picturing your face as you realize what's happening.

Zipping up the duffel bag, I check my phone again. Now it's time. Time for you to pay.

Chapter Eighteen

Nolan

I had to end my old life before I could begin my new one. Of course, knowing that didn't make the task any easier. I waited for two days to break the bad news to Daniella, with the excuse that she had back-to-back nursing shifts and I wanted her full, well-rested attention. I used the time to rehearse my words over and over. But there was no painless way to tell someone you weren't compatible.

The moment came when I got home from work that evening. Sutton was snoring on his favorite armchair, sprawled out like a pudgy beanbag, and Daniella was reading on the couch. She had almost finished the sci-fi novel she'd started a few short weeks ago.

Back then, I had thought that nothing could disrupt our safe, sterile peace. Everything had changed so fast, fallen so completely out of balance. Even if I could bring myself to abandon Lacey now, life with Daniella would never be quite the same.

There was no longer any doubt in my mind about what I wanted. As much as I dreaded this conversation, as much as it would hurt Daniella, I knew that staying in denial would hurt all three of us even more.

Daniella tensed at the sound of my footsteps. As if my nearness hurt her, as if she knew what was coming. But there was no other way. All I could do was make the cut as quick and clean as possible.

"Hey," I called out, as if she didn't already know I was home. "How are you?"

She dropped her book on her chest to look at me. "My day was okay. Sutton was acting crazy earlier, running around and barking at nothing."

"Sutton, running? Are we talking about the same lazy asshole here?" My laugh fell painfully flat.

Daniella shrugged. "I saw him do it. Maybe he thought something was happening outside."

I crossed the room and sat down on the chair's arm. "So, there's, um . . ." Why couldn't I make my mouth work? I tried again. "I have to tell you something."

She blinked slowly. "It's about Lacey, isn't it?"

"Yes." I wondered if she knew what was coming, but I pushed on anyway. "I never intended for this to happen." *Damn it, Nolan, just get it out.* "Things have . . . changed."

She nodded sadly in acknowledgment, waiting for me to continue. But the words stuck in my throat, leaving us in awkward silence for several seconds. Our perfect little bubble had popped, despite our best efforts.

"Do you love me?" she finally asked, her voice whisper soft.

I hesitated, just long enough for the seeds of doubt to grow. "Of course I do."

A single tear rolled down her cheek. "It's okay. I want the truth."

My throat tightened, and I couldn't answer. Couldn't look her in the eye and say the words I knew would crush her. God, this was excruciating. I took a deep breath.

"Then go to her." She wiped the tear away with the back of her hand. "Give her everything."

I had expected shock and confusion, anger and fear, all gushing out in a big, ugly explosion. But Daniella's hazel eyes held only weary resignation. I had never seen her look so purely sad.

Finally, she put her book aside and sat up. "I figured it would turn out this way."

Say what? I stammered, "You . . . did?"

Daniella sighed. It was an empty sound. "Earlier today, Lacey came by to talk. She told me everything." She wet her lips. "I realized that you're . . . in love with her. Like, for real. So I'm glad you're not letting me get in the way of that."

I fought through my surprise, trying to process everything she had just said. Deep in the back of my mind, I felt a faint, shameful gratitude that Lacey had laid some of the groundwork for me. But mostly I just felt like shit. It was bad enough that I was cutting off Daniella—but she had to hear the news from the very woman who'd stolen my heart?

She forged ahead through my conflicted silence. "You're a good man. You've done so much for me. I just want you to be happy, and if Lacey makes you happy, then I understand."

I shouldn't argue with Daniella when she was trying to make this easy. But I couldn't stand the thought of her playing the martyr. I couldn't let her step back into her old, worn role of the cool girl who laughed off every insult, always "up for anything," never inconveniencing anyone with her pain. The good sub who served all her master's whims, who was paraded around in public and ignored at home. The smart, generous, hardworking woman who tried her best . . . yet always ended up left behind.

"I've always known this day was coming," she went on. "Ever since I moved in two years ago. You're a good catch. I knew you'd eventually meet a woman who wasn't okay with sharing." She blinked rapidly, her voice growing hoarse with emotion. "And . . . I've been doing some thinking. In the long run, this is better for me too."

"Daniella, I don't want to hurt you. Where will you—"

"Stop feeling guilty and listen to me."

I shut the hell up. Daniella gave a long, loud sniff before continuing.

"I needed a wake-up call like this. I've been hiding for too long. I let my ex poison my life. I didn't want to see him and his new sub, so I avoided places I once loved. I didn't want to meet another man like him, so I haven't even tried dating for two years."

"But that's okay, isn't it? You needed a break."

Actually, she had needed a safe place to rest her heart. Even now, after so long, she still couldn't bring herself to say that asshole's name.

Her lower lip quivered and she looked away, steeling her resolve. "Yeah, it was okay . . . for a while. But it's time for me to get back on my own two feet. Make a fresh start. Find a way to be truly happy again, not just comfortable. Because sometimes . . ." She took a deep, shaky breath. "*Comfortable* is just another way of saying *afraid*."

Taken aback, I nodded soberly. She had put it into better words than I ever could. I knew what it was like to cage myself in fear. Both Daniella and I had organized our whole lives around avoiding the inevitable, terrified of connection and the risks that came with it. As much as I hated to admit it, we'd been holding each other back. Using each other as security blankets, so that we never had to grow up and move on.

Looking back on the past few years, I couldn't believe how stupid I'd been. I thought I'd singlehandedly discovered the secret to happiness, but all I'd really done was given up trying. It had taken Lacey to make me understand that. To make me see the light.

As Daniella's tears finally started to flow, I knelt and gathered her close. "Come here."

She buried her crumpled face into my shoulder. Her lean body shook in my arms. Normally she stood so tall, so self-assured, exuding an air of effortless grace, but right now she seemed small and fragile and lost. Needing to be taken care of.

Although I could never be her Dom again, I could still offer refuge as her friend. I could still give her this space to fall apart, free from shame or fear. And when she was ready to pull herself together and move forward again, I would be there to help.

I held her tight for a long time. Until her sobs smoothed

out into deep, heavy breaths.

Not knowing what else to say, I mumbled into her hair, "You can keep my damn sweatshirt if you want. I know it's your favorite."

She forced a chuckle. The little *hmph* sound was pathetic and snot-clogged, and for a second, I wondered if she'd be okay without me.

"No, it's yours, and I shouldn't hang on to anything from here, anyway. Fresh start, remember?" She pushed herself out of my arms.

Realizing where she was going, I said, "You don't have to start moving out right now. Lacey would understand if you stayed another week. Or even through the end of the month."

But Daniella was already halfway down the hall.

I followed her into her bedroom. "Where are you going to stay?"

"With my little sister." She grabbed a tissue and blew her nose with a loud honk. "Delphine's been thinking about moving out of her current place. I could be her new roommate."

"I'm sure she'd love that. You'd get to hang out more," I replied. Both sisters shared a fondness for ink and piercings.

Quite a few of their tattoos matched, commemorating travels, graduations, birthdays, funerals.

It wasn't enough for Daniella to live life; she wanted to feel it viscerally, to carry the memories of pain and pleasure on her skin. Would tonight merit a tattoo someday? I hoped it would be a happy one.

We dug through her closet and desk, sorting all her stuff into Take, Leave, and Pitch piles. Along the way, we uncovered random memories, meaningless to anyone except us.

Football hats and foam fingers and ticket stubs from stadiums all over Texas. A DVD box set of a TV series we'd once obsessed over. A pair of scarves that one of Daniella's elderly patients had knitted for us while recovering from surgery. Souvenirs from our road trip when I'd had business in New Mexico: a tiny jar of white sand, a Roswell UFO key chain, a turquoise necklace with an O'Keeffe painting pendant.

"I never knew you were such a pack rat," I grumbled after a couple of hours.

That wasn't really funny, but Daniella chuckled anyway. "Hey, what can I say? I'm a sentimental slob. Or maybe just a regular slob."

I held up a takeout menu with a cartoon chili pepper on it. "Why the hell did you hang on to this? Pepe's Fire Pit went out of business six months ago."

"It was my favorite place; I was sad when it closed down. You know how much I love spicy food."

"Yeah, because you're a masochist." I found another one of my shirts and threw it in the Leave pile.

"Tell me something I don't know." Daniella sighed.

It sounded like she was talking about more than just her kinks. I felt a pang of sympathy; she seemed to keep falling into relationships with men who ended up hurting her. But I needed to focus on the situation at hand and help Daniella get through this, not wallow in my own guilt. I should believe her when she said I wasn't acting like her ex-Dom. She had always taken my words at face value, so I should give her the same courtesy.

"Holy shit, is this that party?"

I showed Daniella a glossy photo whose edges had started to curl. A dozen or so people—mostly women—were grinning and waving in someone's backyard. The barbecue grill stood open, but empty, and three huge delivery pizzas covered the picnic table.

Daniella gave a half groan, half laugh. "Oh God. I'd just transferred to the ER. The head nurse invited the whole department to her Fourth of July party, and your fucking dog made me look like an idiot."

"You still holding a grudge about that?" I chuckled.

In a rare burst of initiative, Sutton had leaped up on the table holding the raw meat, knocking everyone's dinner into the dirt. What little food he didn't devour was ruined. Daniella and I had apologized profusely and paid for pizza with all the trimmings.

As we sorted and joked and reminisced, my shoulders slowly unknotted. The tension that had clouded our home started to ease. We were finding our footing again as friends. *Just* friends.

Even so, I could still hardly believe I'd done it. I'd actually broken up with Daniella. Paradoxically, taking this huge step made me even more nervous about telling Lacey. It brought the future—that terrifying place where everything changed—one step closer.

Tomorrow night, I decided. I would invite Lacey out for a nice dinner and tell her the good news there. Almost like I was proposing.

Before I could explore that thought, my pocket buzzed. I pulled out my phone and my neck prickled when I read the caller ID screen. *Jerry Barton.* Nobody from Redstone ever called me outside work hours, let alone the big boss himself.

Wondering if our office building had caught fire, I answered, "Yes, sir?"

"I've got a job for you, Maxwell. Top priority," Barton snapped, his tone making it clear that refusal wasn't an option.

I had heard that no-bullshit bark plenty of times before. But there was also an unfamiliar urgency in his gruff voice. It almost sounded . . . frantic.

What the fuck was going on here? Barton had never revealed the slightest hint of fear to his men, not even in the worst battlefield situations. If I didn't know better, I'd say he was scared shitless right now.

I started to reply, "Of course, whatever you—"

"It's my daughter, Lucky. She's in trouble."

Chapter Nineteen

Lacey

I had to pee.

As I shifted to my side, pain seared through my hip and up my spine, making my stomach roll with nausea. I gasped aloud—only to choke on the stench of mildew in the air.

What the hell? My eyes flew open.

I wasn't at home in my bed. I was lying on a cold cement floor, still dressed in the red tunic and leggings I'd worn yesterday in my attempt to win over Nolan once and for all. When I tried to lift my arm, I realized my hands and ankles were secured with plastic zip ties.

The darkened room around me was cluttered with sagging, dusty boxes, and an old washer and dryer were tucked into the far corner. A five-gallon bucket stood overturned several feet in front of me. *As if someone had sat there watching me*, I realized with a shudder.

Was I in someone's basement? How long had I been lying unconscious here? The dim light filtering in from the one window told me it was daybreak . . . or maybe sunset. I wasn't sure which.

My mind spun sluggishly to catch up. The last thing I remembered was preparing my apartment for Nolan to come over. I'd lit candles and then changed into a figure-hugging outfit, hoping we'd have *the talk* and figure everything out between us.

At the knock on the door, I'd opened it with a smile, assuming it was Nolan. A man in dark clothes had grabbed me. Shoved something over my nose and mouth until I was close to passing out.

The memory blurred at the edges, my mind still foggy so the details were just out of reach. My heart galloped at the memory. I'd struggled with a man much bigger and stronger than I was, trying to scream, trying to make a scene so that one of my neighbors would notice. But it had all happened so fast. Before I knew it, I was being shoved into the back of a car in the parking lot. The white sedan I'd seen a few times before. A second man in the driver's seat had sped off just as I lost consciousness.

Studying my surroundings, trying to gather up every detail I could, I strained my eyes in the gloom, ears pricked for the smallest sound. But there was nothing.

A chill of dread crept down my spine. This had to do with Troy; I just knew it. And this time, there would be no running away. I had a horrible feeling I was going to die here.

No, no.

I fought back a wave of tears and nausea, forcing myself to calm down and keep listening. My captor was probably upstairs. But I couldn't hear any movement or talking. It was dead silent, only the whoosh of my heartbeat thudding in my ears.

I checked myself over for injuries. Lifting my bound hands, I felt a lump under my hair on the back of my head. *Ouch.* I winced and pulled my hands away from the tender skin. But other than having to pee terribly, I seemed to be fine. For now.

God, I'm such an idiot. Why hadn't I told someone—my dad, Nolan, anybody—about what was going on? Thinking of Nolan made my chest ache and my eyes sting. I wanted him to hold me so badly.

My stupid goddamn plan had failed. He had no idea where I was, and even if he could somehow figure it out, did I even deserve for him to rescue me? I'd fucked everything up beyond belief. One way or another, our relationship was almost certainly over. His life with Daniella would go back to normal, our whole brief affair forgotten.

Heavy footsteps thudded overhead and I froze. My heart pounding, I sank back against the wall, bracing myself for whatever came next.

Chapter Twenty

Nolan

It's my daughter, Lucky. Those four simple words had sent adrenaline surging through me.

Barton had lost too much, seen too much action, and buried too many men over the years. If it was me he trusted to save his daughter, I was sure as shit bringing her back alive, and not in some body bag. At least I'd do my best, and if I died trying, so be it. It was a fair trade, as far as I was concerned. I didn't know much about his children, only that he had two grown daughters he was immensely protective of.

My assignment was simple. Barton had been tracking these assholes for a while. Apparently they were connected with that same Oklahoma City drug ring I'd assisted the police with a few weeks ago. His informant said the kidnappers drove a white sedan and were at a house in North Dallas, near Ridgecrest and Hemlock.

I grimaced; the Five Points area was one of the city's worst neighborhoods. But with a little help from a friend, I'd be more than up to the task.

Daniella had been confused at the sudden interruption, but she understood why I couldn't always share the details about my job. After she wished me luck and resumed packing, I called Greyson to tell him I needed backup. Barton trusted me to build my own team, and Greyson was the best choice. Having spent so many years working closely together, we operated as each other's shadow. I picked him up at his house and debriefed him while we drove to Redstone.

We checked out a pair of handguns and bulletproof vests from the company's armory. Barton had pulled some strings to equip his employees with firearms identical to those they had used in the service. It wasn't just for sentimental value; even after retraining, operating a different gun from the one you were used to could cost precious milliseconds or crucial accuracy. So I got a shiny new SIG P226 Navy pistol. Small enough to conceal, but big enough to kill anything that moved. I could only pray this assignment wouldn't come to that.

Once Greyson and I were fully outfitted, we headed to the intersection of Ridgecrest and Hemlock. From there, we drove in widening circles, keeping an eye out for a building that fit the informant's description. It didn't take long to spot a small, dilapidated ranch house with a white sedan parked out front.

Keeping low, I crept across the overgrown yard to look in the window. I saw a mostly bare living room with mold-stained walls. The single naked light bulb on the ceiling cast more shadows than it banished. A man sat on the couch, hunting knife in hand, watching the front door. The skin on the back of my neck prickled.

This was definitely the right place. I turned my attention to the layout of the room. Its only access points seemed to be the front door and the kitchen. If they had a hostage here, I was guessing she and her guard weren't the only ones present, since Barton had told me the kidnapping was gang-related. More people were probably waiting elsewhere in the house. But how many, I had no idea.

I signaled to Greyson and we moved to the front door. We weren't the police; we had no obligation to announce ourselves or give the enemy a chance to come quietly. We would use the element of surprise to get in and out as fast as possible.

With Greyson close behind me, I shot through the lock and kicked the door in.

The guard jumped to his feet. He took one look at our gear and bellowed, "Cops!"

His warning shout confirmed the presence of his allies. No intimidation tactics, then. Even if I managed to threaten him into dropping his weapon, it would just waste enough time for his buddies to show up. But I also didn't like killing people if I could help it, and I wanted some answers from these assholes.

The guard rushed at me, knife brandished in his fist like an ice pick. *How sloppy.* He pulled back his arm to stab downward, and I spun to let the blade pass in front of me. I grabbed his wrist in one hand and pistol-whipped him in the back of the head. He thrashed and cursed in defiant rage. I slammed his face into the floor, forcing him to his knees, his knife arm twisted painfully behind his back. His snarling quickly transformed into incoherent screeching.

I must have dislocated his shoulder, which meant his knife arm was thoroughly disabled. Unless this prick was ambidextrous, it was time to stop screwing around with him and get what we came for. I holstered my pistol, yanked his knife away, and hauled him onto his feet.

I pointed to a spot along the wall near the kitchen door. "Stay there," I growled under my breath.

He bared his bloodied yellow teeth and spat on my vest. I just stared hard at him, eyes narrowed, and pointed again— with the knife this time. After a moment, he accepted that I wasn't bluffing and obeyed my order.

I flashed Greyson a quick sequence of hand signals to tell him I'd search for the hostage while he stayed behind as a lookout. Grey gave a nod of approval and faced the kitchen, pistol at the ready. The former guard seemed willing to stay down, but Grey still kept one eye on him.

I crept through the kitchen and found a set of stairs that led to a basement. It was rare that Texas homes had basements, but maybe that was why these perps had chosen this house in the first place.

With my back to the wall, I silently crept down. The lower level stank of mildew. A quick sweep of the area showed concrete floors and walls, and a shadowy figure huddled in the corner. It was so small I almost missed it. Even facing the wall, though, it was clearly female.

Shit, the hostage.

She'd better be alive or these assholes were going to answer for this. But as I crossed the room, she gave a small murmured groan, and I released a relieved breath.

I knelt behind her and used the guard's knife to cut through the plastic zip ties securing her wrists and ankles. She made a groggy noise and struggled weakly on her side. She seemed awake, but very disoriented; maybe her kidnappers had sedated her. Or just given her a concussion.

"Don't worry, Lucky, you're safe now," I murmured. Her name had probably never been more appropriate. Once her limbs were free, I rolled her over. "I'm one of the good guys. I'll get you out of . . ."

The words died in my throat. Even in this dim, sickly light, her face was unmistakable. It was Lacey.

Terror and relief tore through me at the same time, leaving my knees weak and my heart pounding. Lacey had been kidnapped by drug-dealing psychos. That realization was instantly followed by another—Lacey was Barton's precious little girl. Any relief I felt was instantly boiled away by anger.

She'd lied to me this entire time? She was Jerry fucking Barton's daughter?

Alerted by the sounds of combat and thundering footsteps overhead, I lifted her limp body and slung her over my shoulder. We reached the top of the stairs just in time to hear Grey's pistol boom. A man tumbled over in a heap, screaming and clutching his knee. The first man reached out to help him, but stopped when I aimed my pistol at him.

"I told you to stay still, motherfucker," I growled.

Keeping his sights trained on the injured man, Greyson crept close and plucked the gun from his belt. He ejected the magazine onto the floor and threw the empty weapon across the room.

With one arm balancing Lacey's dead weight over my shoulder and the other hand on my gun, I forced myself to stay cool. Whatever I might feel about her deception, this job wasn't over yet.

I reevaluated our tactical situation. Two men, both disarmed, one with a busted shoulder and the other with a busted leg. All this fighting had made one hell of a ruckus, but nobody else had shown up. If any reinforcements were on their way, they would have already arrived. So either these two guys operated alone or their allies had bailed at the first sign of trouble.

Seriously? What a fucking joke.

I holstered my pistol, letting my hand linger on the stock. I knew I could draw it faster than these guys could close the distance between us. Cocking my head at the girl draped over my shoulder, I barked at the men, "Do you know who her father is?"

I was wondering what their motivation could be, and exactly how stupid they were. Had they been trying to hold Lacey for ransom? Did they have some kind of grudge against Barton? Or did they just abduct pretty girls and . . . ? I fought down another surge of anger.

Both men just gave me a surly glare. I slowly drew my pistol again, giving them plenty of time to imagine what might happen if they didn't cooperate.

The second guy stayed tight-lipped; his face was white with pain. But the first one muttered, "Who gives a fuck about her daddy? She was Troy's bitch; s'all that matters."

I opened my mouth to ask, *Who the hell is Troy?* Then I remembered. I had come across that name before. Just last week, when I helped the FWPD investigate the collapsed Oklahoma City drug ring.

Jesus Christ. Laccy was a crime lord's girlfriend? No, she *used* to be; Troy had come to a grisly end. But still, I never could have imagined this. When she'd told me that she was running from something, I'd assumed it was a broken heart she'd left back home. Nothing that a bottle of tequila and a rebound fling couldn't fix.

Damn, how wrong I'd been.

I'd assumed these guys were either small-time thugs, attacking randomly, or using Lacey to target her father. But it had been neither. They were after Lacey herself. She knew something, owed them something—or at least, they assumed she did.

The longer I thought about it, the more this entire situation stank. When these guys snatched Lacey, Barton had instantly found out about it; he wouldn't have kept such a close eye on them if he hadn't expected trouble. He must have had some personal experience with this gang in the past.

Barton probably had his reasons for playing it cool, but why hadn't I heard any of this from Lacey? She'd never mentioned that she was in deep shit with organized crime. Or the fact that her dad happened to be my boss.

She'd hidden this information from me. I didn't know why. But I knew she had lied to me. Enough to start a shadow of doubt creeping over our whole relationship.

If there was one thing I couldn't stomach, it was a liar. My entire life was devoted to control, exposing corruption and bringing order to the world. She'd brought all this to my doorstep with an innocent smile and those come-hither eyes.

Anger burned like molten lead in my veins. But I beat it back again; I still had business to take care of here.

"Looks like your lucky day," I announced to the two men with a bravado I didn't feel. "I'm not going to blow your fucking brains out. And if you want things to stay that way, you'll leave this girl alone for good. She's not involved with whatever sick shit you're up to."

Part of me wondered whether that was true. After what had just come to light, how could I be sure of anything? For all I knew, maybe Lacey *had* played a part in Troy's business.

I shook my head, forcing myself to stop spinning in her secrets. We needed to get the hell out of here. There would be time for answers later.

Without taking my eyes off the two men, I said, "Cover me, Grey."

Greyson kept his pistol pointed at them while I adjusted my hold on the limp body over my shoulder. I backed out of the kitchen and toward the front door . . . until I felt a light tap on my back.

"I have to, um, pee," she whispered, her voice hoarse.

My eyes locked with Grey's. "She has to pee," I repeated like a dipshit.

Grey's eyes widened and he shot me a look that said, *Seriously? And if she had to take her tampon out, would you help with that too?*

The sad thing was, yeah, I probably would. I carried her straight into the crappy little bathroom and tugged down her leggings and panties. A bit unsteady, she sat down and relieved herself, her posture slumped in defeat. I averted my gaze, keeping it locked on the doorway, both to give her some privacy and to make sure we were still alone.

When she was done, I scooped her up in my arms and walked out of that foul, run-down house, secure in the knowledge that Greyson was covering me all the way to my truck.

He started the engine as I laid her gently across the backseat and got in, scooting so my lap supported her head. She couldn't sit up by herself, and to be honest, as mad as I was, I needed to hold her.

As Greyson sped toward the highway, I pulled out my phone and dialed the Dallas PD's narcotics division. The bored-sounding officer who answered perked right up when I delivered my tip about a certain drug operation. Those bastards would be going to jail for a long, long time.

When I hung up, Greyson's gaze flicked to the backseat. "Is that really Lacey?"

I grunted an affirmative, in no mood to discuss this with him. I couldn't even wrap my brain around this fucked-up situation yet, let alone put words to it. Trying to make sense of things, I turned and stared out the window.

He blew out a loud breath, nonplussed. "So you've been dating the boss's daughter this whole time? Damn. I don't want to be around when *that* hits the fan."

He probably couldn't see it, but I grimaced at him anyway. "Is that really what you're focused on right now? Jeez, dude, unfuck your priorities."

Although there might have been a tiny part of me that agreed with him. It wasn't enough that she was a drug lord's ex—she had to be the boss's daughter too? That was just icing on the goddamn cake. I'd gotten us away from Troy's old buddies, but would I be so lucky with Barton?

"Drop us off at my place," I instructed Grey.

Barton had said no hospitals unless his daughter was in need of immediate medical care. He said he didn't know how big this thing was, or who he could trust yet. Still in DC when he got the news about the kidnapping, he couldn't have been here quickly enough, so he was counting on me alone to keep her safe. I was only thirty minutes from her, and he trusted me implicitly.

Too bad he had no clue that I'd been eating his daughter's pussy and lusting after her so badly I ached. *God damn it.*

"No . . . Ian . . ."

I startled when a slim hand brushed mine. I looked down to see Lacey gripping my fingers weakly. Her blue eyes were still heavy-lidded, but much brighter than before.

"You really came . . . for me?"

"Of course I did."

She trailed off into a blurry mumble. It might have been my imagination, but I thought she said *I'm sorry.*

"Shhh." I stroked her tangled hair. "It's okay. Just rest."

It wasn't fucking okay, not at all. My doubt was still growing, and with it, my angry sense of betrayal. But for now, I let Lacey sleep—and I let myself enjoy her warm weight, knowing how soon I might have to push it away.

Chapter Twenty-One

Lacey

Only once we were inside Nolan's house, with the door bolted, could I finally relax enough to draw a deep breath. He sat me down on the soft leather sofa and my entire body sagged in relief. The fear and adrenaline from the last several hours drained away; I knew I was safe. *Thank God.* What I didn't know is where I stood with Nolan.

Turning to face him, I opened my mouth to say something, to thank him for saving my life. But the words died in my throat. He was fuming mad, stalking around the living room with a grimace, double-checking his gun before placing it on the dining table.

"You lied to me." His voice was hollow and broken, and I hated the look that I saw in his eyes. I hated myself even more for putting it there.

"I w-wanted to tell you. I wanted to tell you a hundred times . . ." My voice cracked on a sob.

He placed a blanket around my shoulders. But I knew I couldn't read too much into his tenderness; it was only his training kicking in.

"Then why didn't you?" He stood before me, his fists

clenched at his sides, a vein throbbing in his neck.

"Because I couldn't. Would you really have been okay with me telling you I was Jerry Barton's daughter?"

He looked down at the floor.

"I didn't think so." I swallowed. "And even without the romantic connection we had, if I'd told you that I was in trouble, told you everything like I wanted to that first night . . . the first phone call you would have made would have been to my dad."

"Damn right I would have. It would have been the smartest thing to do to keep you safe." He stalked closer. "Do you know what those men could have done to you? Do you have any idea how bad this could have been for you?"

I shuddered. "I know."

"So how about you try explaining this to me again. What in the fuck was going on inside that pretty head of yours?"

"That I was tired of being my father's prisoner. I was twenty-three, and barely allowed to date. Especially not Troy. Dad *hated* Troy. Never wanted him in my life. He kept saying, 'I can tell that boy's a bad egg, young lady, mark my words.' Of course, being forbidden just made me run to Troy faster."

I let out a short, bitter chuckle. "And then it turned out Dad's hunches were right all along. I discovered Troy's secret.

He was deep into some crazy shit. But if I'd admitted that to Dad, that would have been the end of it. I probably wouldn't have been allowed to date or do pretty much anything until I was thirty-five. There was no way I was going to let that happen."

"You were going to fix things with your own two hands," Nolan said. Was that a hint of respect in his voice?

"Yes." I nodded fervently. *If I could just make him understand . . .*

"And I was your backup plan."

My mouth dried up. "Only at first. You became so much more than that. Once I got to know you . . ."

"Was it all fake?" he asked, his tone soft and sad.

"No, Nolan. Of course not."

"Stay put," he muttered.

Turning away from me, he stalked into the bathroom at the end of the hall. I heard cabinets open and jars clinking around. I wondered if his hands were shaking as badly as mine were.

The tears swimming in my eyes threatened to fall. I needed to hold it together long enough to make him understand what he meant to me. To make him see that this was real. I prayed for the right words to come.

Seconds later, he returned carrying a first aid kit. He stopped in the kitchen to grab a bottle of water and a sleeve of crackers from the cupboard before stomping back into the living room. He tossed everything onto the couch cushion beside me.

"Eat. Drink," he commanded, his voice rough.

"Nolan, please talk to me. I'm sorry. I'm so very, very sorry."

He blew out a frustrated breath and grabbed the water bottle to unscrew the cap. "Drink," he said again, thrusting it at me.

Trying to please him, I took a small sip. My parched throat thanked me, and I took a longer swig.

"Did they touch you?"

His voice had softened. As mad as he was, he still cared. Of that I was certain. My heart squeezed in my chest.

I handed him back the water. "No, not like that. They were rough, shoved me around, but I'm okay."

Those two idiots were part of Troy's old crew. I had no idea why they thought I'd have his money or drugs since I was never involved in any of it, but that hadn't stopped them from taking me and demanding to know where his stash was. My fingers went to the bump at the back of my head again. It was still throbbing.

"Let me see," Nolan said, dropping down to kneel before me. Tenderly, he lifted the hair off the back of my neck, and felt the hard knot with careful fingertips. "Let me tend to this." He opened the first aid kit that sat beside me and began removing items. Gauze. Antiseptic.

"Can I take a shower first?" I was desperate to get the stink of that house and those men off my skin.

"Will you be okay alone in there?" He studied me with sharp eyes.

Was he offering to help me shower? No, he'd probably ask Daniella to do it—a thought I couldn't stomach.

"Yes, I'll be fine."

He nodded once. "There are towels under the cabinet. Leave the door unlocked in case you need anything." *In case you collapse*, I suspected he meant.

"Okay." I rose on shaky legs and started toward the bathroom.

"Lacey?" he called out from the living room, where he still knelt on the floor.

"Yes?"

"When you're done in there, we need to talk." His tone left no room for negotiation.

I nodded, my throat tightening. "Just so you know, I was going to tell you everything. I wanted you to come over so we could not only talk about our relationship, but so that I could tell you the truth about my past, who my dad was, everything."

He made a grunted sound that I couldn't distinguish.

Walking slowly and carefully, I paused at the door to Daniella's room on my way. Everything I'd seen in this room that night came rushing back. Her naked body shaking with need. The red welts painted across her skin. The primal look in Nolan's eyes.

Blinking away the memory, I realized that her room was devoid of all personal effects. The dresser and desk were bare; the mattress had been stripped. The closet doors were open, and only a few empty hangers remained.

I heard his footsteps behind me and turned to face him, confused.

"What's going on here?" The place was deserted, as if her intrusion into my life had never happened at all. But of course, my heart still knew it did. "Where's Daniella?" I asked.

"You owe me some answers before we discuss anything." His voice was a rough growl and his fists were still clenched at his sides. He looked broken and sad like I'd never seen him. Fear tightened in my gut, even worse than when that man first grabbed me.

Nolan was right, of course. I owed him the truth. Not to mention the world's biggest apology.

Tears spilled from my eyes. I couldn't control them any more than I could control the rush of words falling from my mouth.

"When I met you that night, I acted like it was all by chance. A single twenty-something woman new in town and enjoying a drink at the local bar. That couldn't have been further from the truth."

I hung my head, my eyes trained on the floor at his feet as I spoke. "Everything about running into you that night had been calculated. I already knew I could rely on you, because my father had told me some of the moments that had defined your life ... private, painful things. But *you* didn't know anything about *me*. That's what made my plan perfect. It would never have worked if you'd recognized me. You just would've sent me back to Oklahoma City, or worse, called my father."

"This wasn't some fucking game, Lacey. Your life was in danger." The low growl vibrating in his throat sent my pulse skittering.

"Of course it wasn't a game. It was my life, my freedom. We all have things in our past we're not proud of. Maybe I was too bull-headed; maybe it was foolish to think I could outrun my mistakes. But you don't know what my life was like before. My father can be . . ." Tears slipped from my eyes, and I took a moment to compose myself.

My only form of rebellion had been dating Troy. When I'd discovered he was running a high-profile executive drug ring, I'd dumped him and moved out. But then two of his "friends" raided my new apartment, looking for the money he owed them—or anything they could pawn to make up the difference. My ex was in some big trouble that wasn't likely to blow over anytime soon.

But since Dad had never approved of him anyway, I wasn't about to go running to him for help. What I needed was a do-over, far away from Oklahoma City, and a good guy on my side, especially when I heard on the news that Troy had been found dead. And according to Dad's stories, there was no better man than Nolan.

I told him everything, starting with the night we'd first met at the bar. God, I'd been so scared, so sure he'd see right through me. Every detail of our time together rushed back with resounding clarity.

"I might have come here for a calculated reason," I finished, "but trust me when I say . . . that changed. The way I feel about you is real."

His face, his kiss, his generous soul, even his maimed heart—everything about Nolan made my skin tingle and my heart race. None of that had been fake.

He gave a disparaging grunt. "How do I know you're telling the truth right now?"

But he was still listening, so I kept rattling on. "I figured that if I could befriend you, win your trust, I could call on you in case my trouble followed me to Texas. I knew your instincts and training would kick in. You wouldn't let anything happen to the vulnerable single woman you'd befriended."

He grunted, acknowledging that was probably true.

"I'm sorry . . . so sorry, for everything." I sobbed, repeating the words over and over again.

Nolan didn't say anything. He just stood there, listening, watching me.

"Go shower," he finally said. "I'm sure you're exhausted. We'll talk more in the morning."

He was right; I was exhausted, even if the clock on the wall only read eight o'clock. But as badly as I wanted sleep, I needed to know where I stood with him. Where *we* stood.

"Why didn't you ever sleep with me?" I wiped the tears from my cheeks, my eyes pleading with his for answers of my own.

Confusion drew a line between his dark brows. "What do you mean?"

"Daniella said that if you hadn't slept with me yet, it meant you had real feelings for me." *Please, God, let it be true.*

"Daniella doesn't . . . ," he started to argue, then stopped. His teeth sank into his lower lip and his tortured gaze met mine. "It never seemed right. You weren't the kind of girl I was used to. I couldn't imagine using you that way . . . holding you down . . . fucking you hard until you screamed. Is that what you wanted?"

My heart thumping in my chest, I stepped closer. "You won't break me, Nolan."

His chin cut to the side as he studied me, not missing a thing. My dilated pupils, my nipples forming hard points in my bra.

"This isn't going to end well," he said.

"You don't know that." My voice was firm, drawing on an inner strength I didn't know I had.

"Go shower," he commanded again.

Balling my fists at my sides, I stood as tall as I could. "I needed protection. Falling in love with you was never part of the plan."

I could have sworn I saw a flash of emotion in his eyes. *Sympathy? Relief?* I wasn't sure, because as quickly as it had appeared, he'd blinked and it was gone. Replaced by that vacant mask he so often wore.

Before I broke down in tears again, I hurried into the bathroom and undressed. Then I stood under the steaming hot water and cried myself sick.

I'd fallen in love with Nolan . . . just as I'd made sure that he would never be able to love me back.

Chapter Twenty-Two

Nolan

I watched the bathroom door swing shut. As soon as I heard Lacey turn on the shower, I stomped into the kitchen and poured myself a shot of whiskey. I wanted to punch the wall until my knuckles bled ... or maybe just sleep for a week. But for now, a stiff drink would have to do. With Lacey safe and temporarily occupied, I finally had time to process everything that had happened tonight. All the secrets that had come to light.

It was in the silence of my kitchen that everything crashed around me. I was in love with Lacey. I couldn't fight or deny the feelings soaring through me. Yet the woman I loved had used me.

Why hadn't she just told me she was in trouble? If she had been honest with me up front—like I'd been with her—I probably would have helped her out. But she hadn't even given me the chance to decide. We had dated for weeks, growing closer by the day, and she somehow never found a good time to air out her past? *Oh, by the way, I forgot to mention my ex ran a drug ring and now his goons are tailing me, and my overbearing father is your boss.*

Clearly she didn't give a flying fuck about what I wanted. Her half-baked plan was more important than my right to make my own choices.

Except that wasn't quite true, was it? Maybe she hadn't cared when she met me, but her apology just now had seemed sincere. She hadn't shied away from the ugly truth, hadn't tried to downplay or rationalize her mistakes. I could tell how deeply sorry she was.

And then she'd said . . .

I knocked back the rest of my shot and poured another.

She was in love with me. And the most fucked-up thing of all? I believed her. I could feel that she was telling the truth. If she really didn't care about me, she would have either abandoned me or tried to guilt-trip me into staying her boyfriend. Instead, she had looked me in the eye and asked me what she should do next. Giving me this new choice couldn't make up for all the choices she'd stolen from me, but it was still a peace offering. An attempt to show that she understood how I felt.

I could tell Lacey that I never wanted to see her again. Hell, I could probably tell her to leave town by sunrise. *It's all up to you*, her remorseful blue eyes had said. *Whatever you need.*

No matter how pissed I felt, no matter how badly Lacey wanted atonement, there was one tie that couldn't be broken:

I loved her back. She had made me feel things I never thought possible. She had shown me so much. Made me want to *risk* so much.

Every relationship was flawed somehow. Nobody was perfect, and putting two imperfect people together wouldn't magically fix them.

I couldn't deny that I still wanted her in my life. And while I hadn't lied to Lacey, I had acted pretty fucking childish—clinging to Daniella, desperately trying to ignore my growing feelings, unwilling to face anything that might shake up my life. Could I really bring myself to leave Lacey just when I'd finally worked up the courage to commit to her?

The fallout from her lies had been bad, no question, but it didn't necessarily have to end our relationship. It wasn't something we couldn't overcome. Provided that Lacey was serious about earning back my trust, and it really seemed like she was . . .

I wanted to give her another chance.

Immediately a weight lifted off my shoulders. This was the right decision; I could feel it. Although I was pretty sure her father was going to freak out. Speaking of which, I owed him a phone call. About thirty minutes ago.

Fuck.

Barton answered on the second ring. "Status?"

"The takedown was a success. Your daughter is safe." I heard a noise that might have been a tired sigh of relief. "She's here with me for the night in my home. And the police should apprehend the kidnappers soon, if they haven't done so already."

"Excellent work, Maxwell. I'll expect a full debriefing tomorrow morning."

Before Barton could hang up, I interrupted. "There's something else, sir." The honorific slipped out, but I didn't correct myself; I needed all the ass-kissing I could muster for this next part. "I, um, didn't know that Lacey was your daughter. I mean, I didn't know Lacey and Lucky were the same person." As soon as the words came out of my mouth, I realized how asinine I sounded.

Evidently Barton agreed. "What the hell are you talking about? Lucky's her nickname."

"Well, it turns out, we kind of . . ."

I rubbed my forehead, which was starting to get damp. This man was well-armed, well-connected, and knew how to use high-powered rifles with deadly precision.

Fuck, I'd rather be back at the drug house getting knifed in the gut.

"We have a history," I finally bit out.

A moment of silence. I swore I could feel the air temperature drop.

Then Barton replied stiffly, "I'm listening."

Oh shit. I had a maximum of ten seconds to explain myself before I was as good as dead. "I met her in a local bar about a month ago. She called herself Lacey, so I didn't know she was your daughter. And we became ... close. Romantically." I almost choked on that last word.

"Why are you telling me this? I fail to see its relevance to your assignment."

I took a deep breath and steeled myself. "It's not relevant, sir. But now that I know she's your daughter, I wanted to ask your blessing to date her."

There was another moment of silence. This one, though, I couldn't read at all.

And then Barton laughed. It was only a chuckle, a short, gravelly huff, but it was still the most laughter I'd ever heard from him. "It's not *my* permission you need, son. Although, for what it's worth, I think my daughter could do much worse than you."

Before I could think of a response, he hung up.

I stared stupidly at the phone in my hand. *She could do*

worse, huh? Coming from Barton, that was pretty high praise. Then again, Troy the dead druggie wasn't exactly a high bar to clear.

"Did you really mean that?"

I startled and turned around. Lacey stood at the entrance to the kitchen, blinking at me, the tentative beginnings of a smile on her lips. She was wearing my thin plaid bathrobe; it hung on her small frame, showing her creamy collarbones and the slightest swell of cleavage. Her wet hair, so dark it looked black, clung in tendrils on her neck and shoulders. Her cheeks were flushed from the hot water. Her eyes were huge, making her look vulnerable, and I had to tear my gaze away before I kissed her.

"Yeah, I meant it," I muttered.

She fiddled with the robe's sash, fighting her grin. "So . . . you still want to be my . . ."

Sighing, I nodded. Her face lit up and I hurried to add, "But I don't know if I know how. With Daniella, I never . . . *we* never dealt in feelings." Or at least, not the depth of emotion I had suddenly found myself drowning in.

"We can learn how to do this together. I know I have a lot of ground to make up for. I should have told you everything from the start; I know that now."

I nodded. "I get that you had your reasons for

concealing the truth. People do strange things when they feel threatened. And besides, you told me in the beginning you were running from something. I chose not to press you. Maybe, unconsciously . . . I wanted to stay in blissful ignorance. Blind myself to anything that could have gotten in the way of us."

"Us. Just us? So Daniella's gone?" Lacey turned her head toward the empty bedroom at the end of the hall.

"She's really gone."

"Are you . . . okay with that?" She chewed on her lower lip, waiting for me to respond.

"Yes. I held on to her for too long. I thought at first it was because she needed me, but in a strange way, I guess I needed her too. It was time."

Lacey nodded. "I understand. You were scared."

I didn't deny her accusation. A big badass SEAL shouldn't be scared of anything. But love? Yeah, that scared the shit out of me.

"I'm not used to being someone's boyfriend. There's a good chance I'll fuck this up." Better that she know that now.

A crooked smile graced her lips. "You're probably better at it than you think." Lacey pondered for a moment. "What's your first instinct right now?"

"To make sure you're okay," I said immediately. *And beat the ever-loving fuck out of those men who touched you.*

"That's perfect." With a gentle smile, she stepped into the kitchen. "I'm a little shaken up, but nothing serious. What would your next instinct be?"

I licked my lips. I could smell the faintest whiff of something familiar; Lacey must have used my shampoo. She was wearing my clothes and my scent. All the hesitant, confused voices in my head suddenly went quiet, letting me hear what I really wanted.

Smiling back at her, I lowered my voice to a whisper. "To take you to bed and not let you out until morning."

My woman stepped forward again, so close I could feel her warmth. "That's perfect too."

She squeaked with surprise when I swept her up into my arms. Leaving my doubts behind along with my whiskey glass, I carried Lacey down the hall to my bedroom, where we had never been together. This was our chance to start over. To empty us both of all our mistakes, all our moments of foolish weakness, and refill each other with our devotion.

For a minute after I laid her on the bed, I just stared at her, enraptured. The robe had fallen open and she lay propped up on her elbows, shapely legs outstretched. She looked like a Renaissance painting of Aphrodite, all alabaster curves and wide eyes and luxurious dark tresses. Delicate, soft . . . and hungry. The shyness in her smile had been overcome by desire.

No man alive could ignore that invitation.

Joining her on the bed, I pulled her into a deep, fiery kiss. My hands pushed under her robe to explore the naked, damp body beneath. I needed to touch every part of her, make sure she really was okay, that she wasn't some mirage. My fingers trailed down her back, along the tender dip where her spine lay hidden, and slid over the curve of her ass. She sighed and opened her mouth to me, brushing my tongue with hers.

I rocked my hips, letting her feel how hard I was already, and she rewarded me with a husky murmur. I licked and bit at her neck—just under her ear, in the crook of her shoulder, all the spots I'd learned to make her squirm.

She mewled softly and clutched at my waist with one hand, rumpling the back of my shirt. I pulled back just enough to rip it off, then pressed my bare chest against her again, reveling in the feel of her velvety skin and ripe breasts.

When she reached down to unzip my jeans, my breath caught. I groaned when she gripped my aching cock through my boxers. She moaned into my mouth. We were flattened against each other so tightly that the back of her hand rubbed her own clit as she stroked me.

I wanted to feel more, wanted us even closer, as entwined as two bodies could get. I needed to lose myself in her. My head spun with her touch, but I still starved for more—torn between the desire to devour her and the desire to go slow, to savor every inch of her body and every sweet noise of pleasure.

"Lacey." I breathed her name into her ear, hot and husky. "I need you." For once in my life, I wasn't afraid to admit it. "Are you sure you're okay?"

All she could manage was a murmured sound of agreement. But I had to hear her say it; there was no going back from this. "Tell me with your words. Are you ready for this?"

Biting her lip, she nodded. "Yes, please. I want to feel you inside me."

I knew from personal experience that traumatic events, like the one she had gone through tonight, left you shaken and vulnerable. But I also knew one sure-fire way to stop those grim images replaying in your head and calm your frayed nerves. Sex—*rough* sex. I wouldn't deny Lacey that pleasure. Even if she was bruised, even if she was still scared, I knew this would help quiet all that, if only temporarily.

I quickly stood up to shed my jeans, grab a condom from my nightstand, and roll it on. Then I knelt between her legs, unhurried. We'd waited so long for this moment; I wouldn't rush it.

She raised her hips to meet me, so eager. Her heat practically burned me through the thin latex barrier.

"Slow, sweetheart."

She seemed to understand. Her hand circled the base of my cock, guiding me forward carefully. I kissed her neck, her breasts, her lips as she brought the head to her wet opening. I couldn't stop my hips from rocking forward, easing into her just the slightest bit.

Her breath caught in her throat and she squeezed her eyes closed, drawing a slow, shaky breath.

"I want you to watch. See how pretty this tight little cunt looks taking me."

Her eyes opened, and she gazed down at where our bodies joined. It was a perfect sight. Two bodies, damp with perspiration, her slick pink folds invitingly parted for my thick cock. I worked myself in another inch.

"So tight . . . so warm." I groaned, bringing my mouth to her neck again and sucking hard.

"Nolan," she cried. "More."

Hips thrusting forward, I slid inside easily. She was so wet for me, so hot and welcoming, that I groaned aloud. "Fuck, *sweetheart* . . ."

She writhed, trying to take me deeper, and I obliged her. Soon my cock had bottomed out. I locked eyes with Lacey as I pulled out, then slowly pushed back inside again, watching to make sure I wouldn't hurt her.

But she was more than ready. "Stop teasing me," she gasped. She was flushed all the way from her cheeks to her collarbone.

I threw aside my careful control and thrust in hard. She keened and bucked up to meet me. *Bingo.* I gripped her hips and started pumping in earnest, making sure to hit that same magic spot each time.

I buried my face back into the crook of her neck, muttering her name like worship against her skin. I couldn't communicate how I felt about her; this was bigger than words, bigger than anything, and I had never really learned how to share my feelings anyway. I didn't even know where to start. All I could do was show her.

For tonight, this pleasure was enough. We would write our love into each other's bodies, where it couldn't be misunderstood.

I pulled her legs up over my shoulders and she moaned

at the new, deeper angle—then whimpered when I rubbed her clit with the heel of my hand. As much as I wanted to stay close, I wanted to make Lacey come even more, which required a little maneuvering room.

Her calves trembled over my shoulders and her fingers dug into the sheets. She was definitely getting close.

"Come for me, baby," I panted. "Please, let me see you." Her pussy fluttered in anticipation and I gritted my teeth, willing my cock to hold off just a little longer.

She stared up at me as if I was her whole world. As if she was trying to tell me that we felt exactly the same way about each other. Then her sapphire eyes slid shut. My name fell from her lips in desperate little murmurs. Her cries keened higher, higher, until all her muscles locked around me and she sobbed with pleasure.

"That's it, baby," I encouraged as she clutched at me, her whole body shaking.

The sight of Lacey unraveling pushed me over the edge. With a deep groan, I let myself fall hard, my cock throbbing in long, sweet jolts of release.

When I could bring myself to let her go, I threw away the condom. Then I spooned behind her, nestling my nose in her still-damp hair and pulling her back against my chest. My arm fit perfectly into the dip of her waist. I could feel her heart beating just inches away from mine.

Soon her breathing slowed into a low, soothing rhythm. I had never made love before; I had never slept with a woman in my arms. It was the deepest peace I'd felt in a long time.

Chapter Twenty-Three

Lacey

I woke up sweating and blinked open one eye. I was hot, way too hot, and I soon found out why. Draped across one side of my body was Nolan's heavy arm. Sutton was snuggled up on my other side.

"Let me up." I shoved against Nolan's prone form.

He grumbled something and scrubbed a hand across his face.

"You okay, baby?" His voice was husky with sleep.

"Yes. I have to pee," I announced, climbing over him to the end of the bed.

I heard him chuckle and the covers rustle as I padded, naked, into the bathroom.

The tiles were cold on my bare feet and the light overhead too bright. Glancing up into the mirror above the sink, I saw that my hair was a crazy mess from sleeping on it damp, but otherwise, I looked fine. There was a faint bruise on my hip, and a pink mark on the inside of my wrist where the zip tie had cut into the skin.

After relieving myself, I washed my hands and splashed

cool water on my face, then headed back to bed.

When I returned to the bedroom, I expected to find a sleeping Nolan and Sutton still curled up on the mattress. But the bed was empty, and they were gone. I could hear Nolan talking on the phone in the other room. It sounded like he was talking to Greyson . . . about last night.

"So they're locked up awaiting trial? No bond?" Nolan asked, and then listened intently. "Great news, brother." He seemed pleased by what he heard.

I could only imagine what kind of strings my dad had pulled; those guys who took me wouldn't see the light of day for years to come. Decades, if I knew my father's reach and tenacity.

I pulled back the covers and crawled into bed. Nolan's spot was still warm and I smiled, closing my eyes.

The scent of coffee brewing in the kitchen wafted into the bedroom. Seconds later, Nolan was back.

"You feeling okay?" he asked, sitting down beside me.

"Yeah. It's only six, though. You're not up at this time of day for the fun of it, are you?"

He chuckled as he stroked my hair, gazing down at me where I rested on his pillow.

"Lord, don't even tell me," I grumbled.

"What?" He practically hummed the word, he was so chipper.

"That you're a morning person?"

He chuckled again. "You're not?"

I frowned at him. *Not even a little bit.*

He shrugged, his mouth still tugged up in a grin. "What can I say? Six years in the military will do that to you. Most days, I was up at four in the morning. Now sleeping in till six feels like a luxury."

I made a noise of disagreement. His bed was too soft, and I felt safe. More comfortable than I'd felt in a long time.

"Come on, I have you here in my house. We have the whole day to ourselves. You really want to sleep?"

"Yes." I tugged the blankets up to my chin and closed my eyes.

Nolan laughed. "Fine, then I won't tell you what your father said last night."

I opened my eyes. *Shit.* My dad was Nolan's boss, and I could only imagine what had been said.

I was sure Dad and Brynn had been blowing up my phone, but since it was likely still sitting on the counter in my apartment, Nolan had let me use his phone last night to check in with them.

I'd promised that I was alive and in one piece. Brynn was an uncharacteristic emotional mess and wanted to fly down to Texas and see me with her own eyes, but midterms were coming up and I wouldn't let her do that.

There was no stopping my dad, however; he'd be arriving tomorrow. I was curious how he'd respond to Nolan in my life. It would be interesting, to say the least . . . two alpha males, both protective and unwavering in their worry for me.

"Fine, I'm up. Now tell me."

Nolan smiled. "He actually seemed okay with us dating. Said you could do worse."

"Of course I could. You're quite a catch." I grinned at him.

"As are you, sweetheart."

We were quiet for several moments. Nolan continued stroking his fingers through my hair while he watched me. I sensed he wasn't going to let me out of his sight for a while, which was fine with me. I had the next two days off from work, and wouldn't mind staying right here in his warm bed the entire time. Realizing how quickly things had changed between us, I suddenly thought of Daniella.

"Is she going to be okay?"

I didn't have to say her name. There was an unspoken awareness that she was still a piece of our puzzle. At least for now.

He nodded. "She and her sister are getting a place together. She'll be fine. She's stronger than I gave her credit for. I just want to focus on you, though. You've been through a lot, baby."

"I know. And I've never felt safer. Being here with you, knowing that you'll protect me at all costs . . ."

"Damn right I will. You're my woman now."

I couldn't help the smirk tugging on my lips. The man who was so deathly afraid of commitment was now openly professing his love. Well, almost anyway; we hadn't quite gotten to those three little words yet. But I knew he was aware how I felt about him after what I'd said last night. God, last night already seemed so far away.

"So, what are we going to do today?" I asked. Lord knew I didn't particularly want to be up at this ungodly hour.

"We have a lot of lost ground to make up for. Real dates. I want to take you to dinner, to meet my mom. Maybe we can visit the ranch where I grew up . . ."

"Whoa. Slow down there." I patted his chest. "I was

thinking more like sex, a shower, and coffee. In that order."

A slow smile uncurled on his mouth. And then he pounced. Bringing his hands to my jaw, Nolan pulled me in for a tender kiss, his body moving over mine. He lay down beside me and drew me into his arms. The warm expanse of his bare chest against mine felt like perfection.

I pushed my hands inside his shorts and found him already hot, hard, and ready in my palm.

"You're mine now. You understand that, right?" he grunted.

"As long as you understand you're mine." I gave him a little squeeze.

A masculine purr rumbled in his throat. "Damn straight, baby." He kissed me passionately, as if his lips and tongue were communicating what words could not. His hot mouth dominated mine, possessive and hungry. "God, if anything had happened to you . . ."

"I'm here. I'm yours."

"Mine."

He grunted again as my hand continued leisurely stroking up and down his generous length. One hand gripped my hip as the other curled between my thighs, lightly teasing, rubbing. Before I could get totally lost in the sensation, I heard a slight wheeze.

I shot a glance over to Sutton, who sat perched at the end of the bed. "Is he going to watch us?"

"Is that a problem?" Nolan smirked.

An elbow to his ribs said *yes, it is.* I was an animal lover too, but sheesh, this was ridiculous.

With a sigh, Nolan got up and shooed Sutton out of the room. "Out you go, buddy." Then he shut the door and returned to where I was waiting, naked, on the bed.

His body was mine to explore now, and I cupped his smooth balls with one hand and stroked his heavy cock with the other, loving his little grunts of pleasure, those male sounds of appreciation rising in Nolan's throat.

"Damn, sweetheart, your hands feel really fucking good," he said on a groan.

I was so happy we'd waited to make love until all the secrets between us had been aired and Daniella was out of his life. It felt bigger, more important, more special now than if we'd given in to our desires before. Now, we weren't just surrendering to our bodies, but making a conscious effort to choose each other, to be together.

Easing one finger into me, Nolan began pushing me toward orgasm almost immediately.

"Make love to me," I murmured.

With a final kiss on my lips, he reached over to his nightstand for a condom.

"I'm clean and I'm on the pill," I blurted.

I wasn't even sure why I'd said it. I guess because I didn't want anything between us, and because I was curious about his status too . . . and whether he'd used them with her.

"I've never been inside a woman without one. Are you sure?" he asked.

It was everything I wanted to hear. We could share something new together.

"Very," I said, my voice growing husky with desire.

"Damn, sweetheart." He groaned again.

And then Nolan's lips were on mine and his hands were in my hair, and his cock was pushing inside me so hot and hard that I lost myself to the blinding pleasure.

Skin to skin. Heart to heart.

• • •

I spent the next two days in Nolan's bed. He fed me comfort food until I was sure I'd gained five pounds, tended to my bruises as they faded, and made sure I was safe, happy, and comfortable.

My dad had flown in for a brief twenty-four-hour stay.

He was busy with work, but he needed to see me with his own eyes, hug me, and make sure I was really okay. And as worried as Nolan had been about dating his boss's daughter, Dad made it crystal clear that he supported us, shaking Nolan's hand and telling him to take good care of me. It was due in large part to what an admirable man Nolan was—my dad seemed to idolize him—but also because of my poor choices in past boyfriends. Nolan was a good man, and there was no arguing that.

We'd also gone over every detail of my ordeal. My dad and Nolan listened while I covered my experience with the kidnappers, recounting everything I could remember. As I spoke, Nolan typed it all into his laptop. He wanted to make sure I had it all down clearly and wouldn't forget crucial details for my testimony, since the trial wouldn't be for a long time. Then we went and gave my statement to the police too, so it was all on official record.

My dad also seemed to ease up a little—letting go of the reins and understanding that this was my life now. I told him I was staying in Texas, and he'd merely nodded.

And now Dad was gone, and Nolan and I both had to return to work in the morning, and back to reality. As good as it had been to stay here with him, I needed to get back to my apartment, back into my life. I didn't want to hide in Nolan's shadow. That was the entire reason I'd come here—I wanted to live, not to cower in fear.

We had finished dinner a short time ago and washed the dishes together in comfortable silence. But even with Daniella gone, there was still something that was bothering me, and I was trying to work up the courage to bring it up to Nolan. Her absence couldn't erase some of the questions I still had.

It wasn't until we were tucked into bed for the night that I found my courage. The room was dark, and Sutton was sleeping in his new dog bed on the floor.

"Nolan?"

"Hmm?" he murmured, running his fingers through my hair while my head rested on his warm chest.

"Where do you keep your toys?"

"Toys?"

"The things I saw that night, the . . ." *God, why does* butt plug *have to be so awkward to say?* "Ropes, blindfolds, and the other stuff."

"Those things belonged to Daniella, and she took them with her. Why?"

He raised his head from the pillow, and I sat up too. I knew he had other interests in the bedroom, and I didn't want to be sheltered from them any longer. If we were going to build a real future together, I didn't want him tempering his tastes for my sake.

"Show me what you like," I whispered, wishing my words sounded as bold as I felt inside.

"You're what I like, sweetheart." He kissed me deeply, his hand at my jaw while his tongue stroked mine.

I pulled back just an inch, placing my hands on his firm chest and rubbing lightly at the taut muscles. "Please. Trust me enough to let me in."

"Not tonight, angel. You've been through too much."

My heart started to pound. "There's this whole other side to you, and I need to know. I need to know I have all of you."

"You do," he said.

"Not like this. I don't want some tame, watered-down version of you. I saw the look in your eyes that night. You shouldn't have to keep that Nolan in check. I need to know *him* if I'm going to be with you."

He let out a frustrated sigh. "You want me to be rough with you? Spank you? Show you all the dirty things I like?"

My heart slamming inside my chest, I nodded.

He kissed me again, his lips searing mine, and I sensed there was an internal battle being waged inside him. Wanting to push him over the edge, I slipped my hand into his boxer briefs and gripped his cock. Then I bit his bottom lip—hard.

Nolan let out a loud growl and flipped us over so that he was on his back, and I was sitting atop him.

"Up on your knees," he said.

The roughness of his voice sent a thrill of adrenaline through me. I rose up on my knees over him, and he shoved his boxers down to free himself.

"I need you to understand one thing," he said as he gripped himself and leisurely stroked. I shivered as his knuckles grazed my clit. "Whatever happened before you has already been forgotten. You're all I want. All I need."

He pulled my panties to the side, his fingers lightly stroking me.

"Soaked for me already. That's my girl." Pulling the damp material down my legs, he discarded them at the end of the bed.

I eased down over him, both of us gasping when he entered me.

"So warm. So snug. So perfect." He grunted as I eased down further. "This is all I want. You. Me . . ." He groaned aloud as I picked up speed, circling my hips to find the depth and angle that made us both cry out. "And if we want toys in the bedroom, we'll pick them out together."

My heart overflowed with happiness. I didn't know those were the words I'd needed to hear, but his answer was perfect. I was enough. Together, *we* were enough.

Soon I was riding him—well, that wasn't really correct. I was on top, but he gripped my waist, shoving me up and down on his cock, using me as his toy. His mouth was everywhere, biting and kissing and nibbling on my breasts and my neck.

I knew tomorrow I would wear his marks, and nothing could make me happier.

Epilogue

Nolan

One Year Later

At the picnic table behind the hospital, Lacey took the brown paper sack from my hand. "Thanks. You're a lifesaver." She pecked me on the cheek.

"No problem, babe." It was my day off, so I'd just been puttering around the house when I noticed that Lacey had forgotten her lunch. "Want some company while you eat?"

"Sure," she chirped, and we sat down next to each other.

As she unwrapped her roast beef sandwich, I took a folded postcard out of my pocket. Its glossy photo showed a stand of golden aspens at the foot of a snow-capped mountain range.

"Check this out. It's from Daniella and Doctor Dom." Lacey chewed while I read the back out loud. "Greetings from the Mile-High City. We're both very busy at Saint Mark's, but we always find time to watch every Texas home game. (Don't worry, we'll never be Broncos fans.) Hope you two have a happy Thanksgiving."

Lacey swallowed her bite. "It's good to hear Dani's doing well."

I nodded in wholehearted agreement. The two women weren't exactly best buddies—my presence had made for too much friction between them—but I knew that Lacey sometimes still felt guilty about breaking us up.

We were both glad that Daniella had finally found her groove in life. A new city to make friends in, and a Dom who loved her and treated her right. Her parting gift had been helping Lacey get a new job at the hospital where she could use her finance degree. Lacey now spent her days on fundraising, working with large donors and securing future investments for the new children's wing of the hospital.

"This last year's been crazy, right?" she asked, setting down her sandwich.

I nodded again, more grimly this time. The men responsible for Lacey's kidnapping were currently serving twenty-five to life. *Good fucking riddance.* Their drug ring charges, on top of armed kidnapping and a whole list of other shit, got them the maximum. That, and Jerry Barton was old college pals with the judge.

"God, if you and Greyson hadn't come that night . . ."

"We did. And you're safe. And you've called and thanked Greyson about a thousand times since then."

She sighed. "He doesn't come around much anymore."

It was true. Since I'd fallen in love and my life became a picture of happy, domestic bliss, he'd backed off a little. I still saw him at work, we still went for drinks occasionally at West's, but he often declined to come over for game days, saying that I should spend my spare time with Lacey.

"Grey's even more fucked up than I was about love," was all I said.

"Geez, what's with you two? Is love really so scary?"

I didn't tell her the whole story about how and why we lost Marcus. Greyson had run that mission and still blamed himself for his death. I hadn't told her because it wasn't my story to tell. But that, along with some other tragic events, had fucked us both up pretty good.

Lacey didn't pry further, and when I stroked her cheek, she leaned into my touch, releasing a soft sigh. She was safe and we were happy. And I hoped that with a little time, and maybe the right woman, Greyson would find his happy place too.

She reached back into her bag and paused. "Hmm? I didn't pack a dessert, did I?"

My heart tripped. She had found the extra container I'd hidden in her lunch. I tried to stay cool as she took out the little plastic box and opened it. Inside was a chocolate cupcake from her favorite bakery—topped with a glittering diamond ring.

Lacey stared at the ring blankly for a second. Then she took a sharp breath and looked up at me, her lovely eyes wide. "This is . . . you really mean it?"

I laughed. "Of course I do. Why do you sound so surprised?"

"It's just that . . ." Setting aside the cupcake, Lacey glanced away, her expression caught between joy and regret. "After everything I put you through—"

"Hey, now," I interrupted, taking her hand. "I understand why you did what you did. And I know you've learned from your mistake. I know you'd never lie to me again."

She immediately shook her head. "Of course not, but—"

"Then there's no buts. I love you, I trust you, end of story." I kissed her knuckles gently, then went down on one knee, still holding her hand. "So . . . Lacey Barton, will you marry me?"

She pressed her other hand to her mouth, her eyes brimming. "Yes!" she said with a laugh.

My heart overflowed. I leaned in to hug Lacey tight and claim my first kiss as her fiancé. Nothing could compare to this moment. I had the world's most amazing woman in my arms . . . and she wanted to be mine forever.

When we paused for breath, I asked with a smirk, "You know what this means, right?"

She blinked, briefly perplexed, then giggled. "Yes, yes. I'm finally moving in with you."

For the last six months, I had asked her roughly a dozen times if she would move in with me. She had always changed the subject or demurred politely, saying things like "Isn't it too soon for that?" and "Oh no, Dad would flip out." While my boss could be old-fashioned—and Lacey had already stressed him out plenty last year—I didn't think Barton was the kind of man to have a heart attack over a little cohabitation.

"So why *did* you keep turning me down?" I asked. I wanted to hear the real reason, in her own words.

She sighed, although she was still smiling a little. "I had two reasons, but they're kind of related. They'll probably sound stupid when I say them out loud."

I got up to sit beside her. "I'm not going anywhere."

"Okay. Well, first, I wanted to make sure I was . . . worthy of you." When I opened my mouth to protest, she put up her hand. "Before I came here, I'd never lived alone before. I've always had roommates, or lived with Dad, or . . . Troy. And after what happened last year, it became even more important for me to learn self-reliance. To be confident that I could deal with my own problems. If we lived together, it would be too tempting to depend on you, and I wouldn't learn anything about myself. I'd just be relying on you."

"But you're amazing in your own right," I teased. "It doesn't matter who you're with."

She smiled despite herself. "Thanks, Nolan. For what it's worth, I think you do make me a better person. But not in an unhealthy way, if that makes sense. You're not a crutch, or my 'other half,' or whatever. I wanted to find out whether I was a whole person who really brought something to our relationship. Does that make any sense?"

I rubbed my chin. "I think so. You want to be with me because you *want* me, not because you *need* me."

Smiling, she nodded quickly. "That's exactly it. Us being equal partners is really important to me."

I reached my arm around her shoulders to give her an encouraging squeeze. "And your other reason?"

"I also . . . wanted to give you your space. I know you were the one asking to move in together, but I couldn't bear the thought of you ever feeling trapped again." She dropped her gaze and bit her lip. "Some part of me was secretly afraid that, one day, you'd come to your senses. And if we were living together, that would make it a lot harder to do what was right for you."

"You mean dump you?"

Her voice was very small. "Yeah."

I brought my other arm up to hug her. "Sweetheart, it means a lot to hear you care so much about my feelings. But managing them isn't your job—I can handle myself." I took her chin, turning her face toward me. "And I'm not sure how I could ever fall out of love with you."

Before I met Lacey, I had thought I was taking life easy. But it wasn't really an easy life if I had to work so hard to maintain it—building my walls high, suspicious of any surprise, shunning any connection that might demand too much. Like living as a guest in my own home, afraid to touch or peer too deeply into anything.

Lacey had shown me how good it felt to drop those inhibitions. To be caught off guard, to lose control, to let life wash over me with all its messy entanglements and contradictions. Being with her, I realized what *home* was supposed to feel like.

She held out her hand and I slipped the ring onto her finger. I wasn't much of a jewelry guy, but the sparkly rock on her slim finger was stunning. Even more so because of what it signified. She was going to be mine forever.

Then I kissed her again tenderly, taking my time and luxuriating in her warmth. Whatever this life threw at us next, I couldn't wait to share it with Lacey—my biggest surprise, my best contradiction, my brightest light.

She'd been the one running, but somehow she'd chased away all my demons and forced me to see what was right in front of me. We'd saved each other in the process, and now she was mine. And I was hers. A thought that didn't scare me, but instead made me feel whole.

"I love you," I whispered, bringing her mouth to mine to steal one more kiss.

Author's Note

This story is unconventional, and that was intentional on my part. Thousands of romance novels are published every year, and many follow the same formula. As a reader, I always get excited when an author takes a risk and writes something outside the box, or reimagines an old concept, breathing fresh life into it. My hope is that you enjoyed this story and that it was a unique experience for you. I am happy that I got to tell it.

While writing this book, I experienced my own traumatic life-threatening event. I haven't talked about it with many people, but I'm ready to share it now with you. One afternoon last fall, I was followed, stalked, and threatened by a man who—the only way I can say it—went crazy and came after me. I had to call 911, and I honestly feared for my life.

I like to think of myself as a tough cookie, but in that moment, while trying to get away from him in my car, I was also trying to explain to the 911 operator what was going on, give her my name, a description of the man, etc. My voice was wavering and my heart was beating a million miles a minute. I did get away safely, after about a ten-minute ordeal, and the man took off and left before the police arrived.

It was only later, when I was safe at home with my husband, that I reflected on this incident. This book, which was about ninety percent done at the time, popped into my mind, and the correlation was easy to make. I honestly felt like I was Lacey and my husband was Nolan. He was my protector, and I felt safer in his arms than anywhere else. He'd kick anyone's ass for me and would never let any harm come my way. Instead of just writing about heart-pumping adrenaline and fight or flight response, I had lived it that day.

Lacey arguably makes some strange choices, but those became clearer to me too. When you feel threatened, common sense is overshadowed by something more primal. You might make different choices than you anticipate.

After this event happened, I considered posting about it on social media, as I do with most major events in my life. I'm a writer; it's what I do. Putting words down to explain exactly what happened sounded therapeutic in some ways, plus I enjoy keeping my readers updated with my life.

But this felt too personal. Too, I don't know . . . delicate. So I chose not to say anything at all.

I will tell you it's changed me in some ways. I don't take things for granted, I hug my babies tighter at night, I check the locks on my doors more often. But I promise you, I am okay. Many people—some of you reading this, I'm sure— have dealt with much worse. My heart goes out to you.

(That's another reason I didn't want to say anything; I didn't want to sound like a drama queen or a whiner.)

Thank you for reading. And thank you for being there for me. I'm learning to appreciate every little thing, and one that's most dear to me is you, my readers.

Coming Soon in the Alphas Undone Series

Slow & Steady

When former Navy SEAL Greyson Archer tosses a twenty on the stage of a strip club, the last thing he expects to see is a pair of familiar haunted green eyes staring at him. Finley should be home raising her infant daughter and baking cookies, not tucking singles into her G-string and giving lap dances.

Greyson can't deny that he'd like his own private show, but there's not a chance in hell of that happening. The last time he saw her she was dressed in black, holding a folded flag and sobbing that it was all his fault—and he'd agreed with every single word. He couldn't do anything to help her then, but he can now.

Finley deserves better than this dingy club, and when an obsessed customer crosses the line, Greyson leads the rescue and will do whatever it takes to make amends for their broken past.

He never expected to want to settle down, but with Finley, everything is different. For the first time ever, he can breathe. But Greyson will have to fight for what he wants in order to keep the woman with the green eyes he's dreamed about so often.

Acknowledgments

To my developmental editor, Angela Smith, wow. You read some pretty crappy first drafts of this book and you still believed in it, which is pretty dang amazing. Thank you.

To Alexandra, your help was both superb and timely. Thank you for everything!

Melissa K., thank you for beta reading an early version of this story and helping to point out the weak spots.

And Pam Berehulke, as always, you rock my world, lady. Editor extraordinaire.

My very own Nolan, you might not be an ex-SEAL, but you're my hero all the same.

About the Author

A *New York Times*, *Wall Street Journal*, and *USA TODAY* best-selling author of more than twenty titles, Kendall Ryan has sold more than a million e-books, and her books have been translated into several languages in countries around the world. She's a traditionally published author with Simon & Schuster and Harper Collins UK, as well as an independently published author.

Since she first began self-publishing in 2012, she's appeared at #1 on Barnes & Noble and iBooks charts around the world. Her books have also appeared on the *New York Times* and *USA TODAY* best-seller list more than two dozen times. Ryan has been featured in such publications as *USA TODAY*, *Newsweek*, and *In Touch Weekly*.

Other Books by Kendall Ryan

UNRAVEL ME Series:

Unravel Me

Make Me Yours

LOVE BY DESIGN Series:

Working It

Craving Him

All or Nothing

WHEN I BREAK Series:

When I Break

When I Surrender

When We Fall

When I Break (complete series)

FILTHY BEAUTIFUL LIES Series:

Filthy Beautiful Lies

Filthy Beautiful Love

Filthy Beautiful Lust

Filthy Beautiful Forever

LESSONS WITH THE DOM Series:

The Gentleman Mentor

Sinfully Mine

STAND-ALONE NOVELS:

Hard to Love

Reckless Love

Resisting Her

The Impact of You

Screwed

Monster Prick